"I'd rather have you," she murmured

Suzanne tried to explain to Owen about putting him in her article. She wished he would look at her. She'd never met anyone like him before. She leaned closer and touched his arm. "I spoke to my editor this morning and told her about you and your life here. And how the Bliss ladies have a matchmaking list and that your name is at the top. She was fascinated."

"Say that again," he whispered, then drew even closer.

"She was fascinated."

Owen shook his head. "No, the first part."

Suzanne smiled at him. "I'd rather have you?"

"That's a dangerous thing to say to a man," he said as he wrapped his arms around her and gazed deeply into her eyes. "Especially one who's at the top of the Bliss ladies' matchmaking list."

And before she could laugh, he kissed her purposefully, with every ounce of passion that he possessed.

Dear Reader,

I often wish the days of matchmakers and mail-order brides would return. I know it's a romantic notion that has no place in the new millennium. But I like to think that somewhere there are matchmakers who know their stuff, so I invented Bliss, Montana, and its enthusiastic Hearts Club members. Edna, Louisa, Missy and Grace aren't shy about finding mates for those who need them. So, matchmakers everywhere, if you exist outside fiction, let me tell you about my sons.

Son #1, age 29, needs a lively, organized lady, one who loves loud music, old dogs, bass guitar players and ancient Nebraska farmhouses. She'd better have a sense of humor, and, of course, if she adores her future mother-in-law's novels so much the better.

Son #2, age 24, requires an intelligent, talkative, domestic young woman. She'd better like Willie Nelson songs, Larry McMurtry novels, cowboy boots and pickup trucks and should be prepared to share a future Hollywood home with six children, 492 videos and a pack of small, fluffy dogs. Once again, a sense of humor and a love of romance novels will add to her (and my) future happiness.

A Wife for Owen Chase was great fun to write and I am now busy on the sequels. Edna Bliss has a few more matchmaking challenges in front of her, but she's not a woman who gives up easily. (And neither am I, so if you know my perfect daughter-in-law, feel free to write to me. If nothing else, we'll have a few laughs and brag about our kids.)

My love to you all,
Kristine Rolofson
P.O. Box 323
Peace Dale, RI 02883

Kristine Rolofson
A WIFE FOR OWEN CHASE

HARLEQUIN®

TORONTO • NEW YORK • LONDON
AMSTERDAM • PARIS • SYDNEY • HAMBURG
STOCKHOLM • ATHENS • TOKYO • MILAN • MADRID
PRAGUE • WARSAW • BUDAPEST • AUCKLAND

For all of my friends in Montana

ISBN 0-373-25942-5

A WIFE FOR OWEN CHASE

Copyright © 2001 by Kristine Rolofson.

This edition published by arrangement with Harlequin Books S.A.

® and TM are trademarks of the publisher. Trademarks indicated with
® are registered in the United States Patent and Trademark Office, the
Canadian Trade Marks Office and in other countries.

Visit us at www.eHarlequin.com

Printed in U.S.A.

1

"No one in Bliss needs a wife more than Owen Chase." Ella Bliss, proud matchmaker and direct descendant of Horace Bliss, the town's founder, tossed the two of clubs into the middle of the damask-covered card table. She and her sister, Louisa, were hosting their weekly game of hearts this Thursday, the second day of November and the first official day of the festival. "He should be our first priority."

"I can think of others, Sister," Louisa snapped, more petulant than usual this afternoon. "Quite a few of them, in fact."

"There are so many deserving young men in the county," Missy Perkins declared. "I don't know how we'll pick this year, but I'm sure we'll find deserving candidates. We always have." Forever the peacemaker of the foursome, Missy was also the youngest, being only seventy-six. The fact that her sweetness was genuine kept the others from eliminating her from the weekly Hearts Club.

"But Owen should be first." Ella wasn't about to give up. She had a stake in this one, having known the boy's grandmother and mother all her life. They would want the fine young man to be happy. "A more lonesome young rancher has yet to be found anywhere in Montana," Ella added, almost forgetting to watch the cards being played.

Grace Whitlow, retired teacher of home economics, took the trick with an ace of clubs, then threw out a low spade. "Poor Owen. He's not the most handsome man in town, but the children deserve—and need—a mother."

"But not just anyone will do," Ella warned. "Only the best for the Chase family. Louisa and I grew up with his grandmother, you know."

"We grew up with every senior citizen in Montana," Louisa grumbled. "That doesn't mean we have to find wives for their grandchildren."

"But that's the point of the festival, dear," Missy said, dropping the card that no one wanted into the center of the table. "Sorry. The queen was the only spade I had."

"No matter." Ella didn't want the extra thirteen points added to her score, of course, so she selected a low spade to discard, then waited for Louisa. Her younger sister's lips turned downward. She really should have put on some lipstick, Ella thought. Louisa was only seven and a half minutes younger than her twin, but when she forgot her lipstick she looked seven and a half years older. She was also plump where Ella was spare, round where Ella was all angles, and the dissimilarity between the twins didn't end with their physical attributes. Louisa had their mother's softness, while Ella took after their father, a tall, rangy man who'd run the town and three businesses until the day he died, sixteen years ago.

"So, do we have any prospects?"

"How about the young lady who took over the bakery? She seems nice enough," Grace said.

"And she can cook," Missy added. "I'm going to order pies from her for Thanksgiving, I think."

Since Missy's piecrusts were known to be as tough as an old turkey, the rest of the women nodded their approval of their friend's decision.

Ella shook her head. "The baker has two little girls of her own to raise and a business to run. With all of her responsibilities, I'm not sure she'd be right for Owen."

"What if we look for a redhead?" Missy suggested. "The baby has red hair. It would be awfully nice if her new mother did, too."

"A redhead," Ella mused, ignoring her twin's frown. "Are there any single women with red hair in town?" She quickly ran through her mental list and came up with no one at all. "Perhaps it's more important that she likes children and is a domestic kind of woman."

"Someone like Maggie Moore, only younger," Grace said.

Missy sighed. "What *are* we going to do about Maggie?"

"And Gabe," Grace added. "Don't forget about him."

"First things first." Ella didn't want this conversation to get off track. "Owen Chase needs a wife. If there's no one in town now, there will be soon. We can look on Friday, when we have a nice group from which to choose."

"The potluck dinner is my favorite part of the festival."

"Mine, too," Grace said, "though I do love the dance. I bought a new dress."

"Stuff and nonsense," Louisa muttered. "That's all it is."

"All what is?"

"Matchmaking. The festival. Everything." She stared at her cards, oblivious to the identical looks of horror cast her way by her friends and her twin.

"My, my," Ella drawled. "Aren't we in a mood today."

"What on earth?" Grace interjected.

Missy leaned forward. "Are you having one of your headaches, Lou? If you'd like to lie down instead of playing hearts, none of us would mind, I'm sure."

Ella would mind. Leave it to Louisa to spoil a perfectly good hand of cards. "You have to discard," she told her. "It's your turn."

Her sister tossed the ace of spades into the pile and took the trick, along with the dreaded queen. She didn't appear to notice, though, which was unlike her. Louisa usually played with the ferocity of a pit bull. Lou then set her cards facedown on the table and faced her twin. "Something isn't right this year."

"Not right? Whatever are you talking about?" Ella felt a moment of panic. Had the festival been canceled without her knowledge? Was there an early blizzard coming across the plains toward Bliss?

"Never mind. It was just a feeling, that's all." Her lips tightened, and Ella recognized the set of Lou's jaw. That stubborn streak ran in the family. Ella turned to Grace.

"Louisa has been puckish with me since she woke up this morning. We ran out of her special tea."

"I ordered it weeks ago from the Harney's catalog," Lou said. "It should have arrived by now."

"Ah," Missy said. "The jasmine blend?"

Ella sighed. "Does she drink anything else but?"

"Coffee gives me a headache." Her sister picked up her teacup and took a sip. "And this herbal tea has no taste."

"Put more sugar in it." Ella felt her patience waning. She wanted to play cards, she needed to discuss various potential matches for Owen, and then there was the dilemma of what to do with a couple of the other bachelors, too.

With Lou's headaches, pouting and general irritability, Ella decided this afternoon's gathering wasn't as entertaining as usual. Maybe it was the oncoming darkness, or the chill in the air that warned that winter was fast approaching. Maybe it was the ache in her old bones that made Ella long for her bed and a glass of bourbon. She glanced at her watch. "He'll arrive at four. He's coming for tea."

Louisa sighed. "I do so hate not having the jasmine blend. Do you think he'll bring the child?"

"What else would he do with it?"

"I do hope he brings her," Lou said, having a soft spot for babies that Ella didn't share.

"We'll do our best for him this year. The baby needs a mother," Ella concluded, and the other three didn't object. "We must put our heads together and come up with some possibilities. After we finish our coffee, we'll make a list."

Missy cleared her throat. "Owen hasn't been to the festival in years."

"He will come this year. The man must be getting desperate by now." Ella glanced at her sister, whose expression remained grumpy. "Speaking of desperate, I want to play cards. Do you?"

"I suppose." She picked up her cards and halfheartedly tossed the king of spades onto the table. "I'm simply not feeling very romantic this year."

"You're eighty-one, Lou. Precisely *how* romantic do you expect to feel?"

Louisa shrugged her shoulders. "I suppose...never mind."

"Go ahead, dear," Missy urged. "You suppose what?"

"Maybe if..."

"If what?" Ella almost snapped. Really! They were never going to finish this round of cards, and here she sat with a hand that fortunately shouldn't leave her holding any points when the round was over.

"Perhaps I'm too old to make matches," her twin said. "Remember 1987? I was so sure that Dick Babcock and Sally Martin would work out, and here they got divorced last month. I find that depressing."

"Mistakes happen," Missy assured her, then prompted the others. "Isn't that right? We've all had our share. And I remember thinking Dick and Sally would work out, too. Who'd have thought she'd run off with the UPS man?"

"Dick Babcock was an idiot." Ella had no patience for idiots. She'd known too many in her day. She'd even fallen in love with one. "Good for Sally, I say."

Louisa sighed. "At least her packages will arrive on time."

Missy shot Ella a confused look, so she explained

that Lou was thinking once again of her missing jasmine tea.

"I'm worried that I've lost my touch."

"You simply woke up in a bad mood this morning. Maybe we should have our dessert now," Ella suggested, giving up on the game completely. Besides, there were more important things to think about than the Babcock divorce and lost tea.

Clearly, Louisa would be little help this year, so, as in most things, it was up to Ella Bliss to solve the problem of finding a wife for Owen Chase.

SUZANNE GREENWAY, jilted bride and born-again cynic, had no business working for *Romantic Living* magazine. Her mission was simple: go to Montana and gather information for a feature story on the most romantic town in the West. In other words, her boss had said, "Find a man who's looking for a wife and follow him around."

Suzanne thought the whole thing was silly and, if she really thought about it, a little frightening. Desperate cowboys and even-more-desperate women all crowding into some dusty little town in the middle of nowhere didn't sound very romantic. She preferred candles, champagne and vintage Sinatra...or she used to. Now Suzanne preferred being alone with a decorating magazine and a bag of cookies—

both easier to acquire than a man, and a heck of a lot more reliable at the end of a long day.

She rented a sport-utility vehicle at the Great Falls airport and headed north, toward a town nestled on the plains at the foot of the Rocky Mountains. Not exactly a resort destination, but Suzanne supposed it had a certain earthy charm. It had the look of a television set, or the background of a country-and-western music video.

She didn't know what to expect, exactly. Women in bonnets waiting to be auctioned off? Potbellied men looking for someone to cook their dinners and warm their sheets? Or would this turn out to be a Western version of spring break, with hordes of oversexed college students looking for as many one-night stands as they could get?

She shuddered. She'd wanted the assignment on Thanksgiving celebrations. But next year's November issue of the magazine would feature tidy New England inns and their tasteful holiday traditions, written by senior editor Paula DeLangue. It would also have an article—complete with color pictures Suzanne would take herself—of "romantic" Bliss, scene of Montana's annual Matchmaking Festival. Or, as Suzanne told her friends in New York, "the cowboy orgy."

And she certainly wasn't in the mood for a townful of romantic pretenders looking to make a buck on quickie weddings and silly tourists.

"This your first time?" The elderly man at the gas station, a man who looked too old to be working outside in such a wind, filled her rented SUV with gas. She could have waited until morning, and she really didn't need gas, the tank being more than half-full, but she wanted an excuse to stop at the edge of town. She had the strangest feeling that once she officially arrived in Bliss, she would be trapped.

"First time?" she repeated, unsure if she'd heard him correctly over the wind.

"For the festival. You a bride or a matchmaker?"

"Neither." She handed him the platinum credit card and then made a careful notation on the back of an envelope. "RoLi" wasn't known for its generous expense accounts.

"You'll attract your share of attention, missy," the man said, winking at her from under the brim of a faded brown Stetson. "You'll have to beat the men off with a stick, that's my guess."

"I don't—" she began to argue. But the man— "Hal" was embroidered on his faded blue jacket— had already headed toward the door of the gas station. Suzanne rolled up the window and shivered. It was almost dark, and from the chill wind whipping around the car she wondered if it was going to snow tonight. She liked snow, as long as it didn't stop her from getting where she wanted to go.

When Hal returned, he handed her a receipt and her credit card, and wished her luck finding a husband. "I'm searching for a wife myself," he offered. "My missus has been gone for four years and a man gets lonely."

"Well," Suzanne said, unsure of what to say. Was the man hinting at dating her? "I wish you luck, too, but I'm here on business, not to get married. I work for a mag—"

"You'll find a man," he assured her. "Pretty girl like you won't have a bit of trouble. Stay away from the heavy drinkers and don't let the wild ones talk you up too sweet. Keep your wits about you and you'll find yourself a good husband, all right."

"I'd rather find 311 Elm Street," she said, wishing she'd turned her tape recorder on so she could quote Hal's advice for the article. "Am I close?"

"Ah," he said, winking at her again. "The Bliss sisters are expectin' you, are they? Well, you'll turn left at the second light and look for the biggest house on the block. It's a fancy place, so you can't miss it."

"Thank you."

"Good luck with the husband hunting, missy. I'm sure I'll see you again," Hal said, and waved goodbye with a gloved hand. Suzanne waved back, then pulled back onto the main street through town driving as slowly as she dared. Even at dusk—especially at dusk—it looked like the setting of every Western movie she'd ever watched with her father, who'd been a loyal John Wayne fan. A wide banner stretched across the street, its fabric secure against the wind. Welcome to Happily Wedded Bliss, it said.

She would get a picture in the morning.

Lights shone from the buildings and storefronts, lit the boardwalks, twinkled as if it was New Year's Eve instead of November 2. A line of people stood outside of a movie theater; another crowd huddled in front of a restaurant that took up half a block. The Bliss Bar and Grill looked like it was doing a good business; the barbershop and the J.C. Penney's were still open. Pickup trucks were parked along the side of the street and a policeman stood on the corner of the second block. He smiled down at two young women and then pointed across the street to a surprisingly elegant coffee shop.

Suzanne stopped at the first red light and stared at the bustling town. Men were everywhere—tall ones, short ones, husky men and lanky men, young, old and in between. They wore Stetsons and heavy coats with sheepskin collars; they walked alone or in pairs. They hesitated before crossing the street to a place called Marryin' Sam's; they lit cigarettes with cupped hands and watched the women who were passing by.

And there were plenty of women in Bliss, she noticed, as the light turned green. She accelerated slowly, letting a trio of thirty-something women finish crossing the street before she moved the car. Clearly, the town was ready for a party, despite the cold temperatures. Suzanne watched with fascination as two tall cowboys sauntered up to a huddle of young women and tipped their hats to them. Amazing, she thought, for courtship to be so blatant.

What on earth caused everyone in this part of Montana to want to get married? She supposed it was her assignment to find out, but she didn't think she was going to understand it when she did.

MELANIE CHASE MCLEAN HAD thighs like a sumo wrestler and a pout that made her uncle want to give her the world. Unfortunately, the only thing Owen had to give her was a bottle of formula, which he hoped would make her smile at him again before he plucked her from her car seat and took her inside the Bliss mansion.

"Here, darlin'," he said, popping the bottle into a mouth prepared to scream her frustration and hunger to the whole world, or at least her little corner of it. Owen's corner was bigger than most, a cattle ranch that took up a fair share of the county. He lived on the Chase Ranch, as had his grandparents and great-grandparents and great-great-grandparents. A few years ago, before she'd gotten sick, his sister had attempted to trace the family's genealogy, and claimed it made her dizzy. There'd been too many Chases to sort out. Uncles and aunts had grown old and passed on, cousins had grown tired of ranching and drifted away to disappear into city life. His father had died in his sleep, here on the ranch in the same room in which he'd been born. And Owen's mother joined him five months later.

Yet here they were, with the prolific Chases having dwindled down to Owen and two girls. They were the last of the line, unless Owen woke up one morning to find a wife sleeping beside him in the king-size bed.

Little chance of that, he knew, unbuckling Mel's seat belt. Her chubby fingers gripped the bottle, making her uncle's contribution to the process unnecessary, but Owen didn't mind sitting in the truck a little longer. The Bliss sisters had called him to town, and he had too much respect for them to refuse the invitation. Besides, he needed to buy groceries and pick up Darcy from basketball practice.

He knew what they wanted, though. He would be on their list again this year, with the other hard-core bachelors the funny old women considered a challenge to their matchmaking talents. There was no way to avoid the meeting with Ella and Louisa, but bringing Melanie along with him guaranteed the visit wouldn't last too long.

Owen waited for the baby to finish the bottle, though patience wasn't one of his virtues. The Chase men were hard-working, stubborn, dependable and...impatient. There was always work to do, and that was part of life in Montana. Owen wouldn't have it any other way, except maybe for this afternoon. He had a lot more important things to do than drink tea and make polite conversation about this year's festival.

So he sat in the truck, his breath fogging the inside of the windows as Mel finished her bottle, then tossed it aside to roll onto the floor. Owen left it there and eyed his niece, who finally smiled at him. Milk dribbled down her fat chin, so Owen took his handkerchief from his jacket pocket and wiped her face clean before he opened the door. He took a deep breath of the cold air before he walked around to open the passenger door. He'd grown accustomed to hauling Mel around; most of the time she was pretty good company. She didn't mind listening to his old Willie Nelson cassettes, and she liked to ride in the truck. Most places they visited contained a middle-aged woman or two who volunteered to keep her busy while Owen conducted ranch business.

Women were helpful creatures. At least, the older ones were, he'd discovered these past months. He lifted Mel into his arms and protected her face from the wind by tucking her against his chest.

And sometimes women could be *too* helpful, he knew, striding up the Bliss sidewalk and up the front steps to the biggest stone porch in the county. When Ella and Louisa opened their front door, he would be greeted with the usual question: "Why haven't you found a wife yet, Owen Chase?"

Because I'm too big. Too quiet. Not that good-looking. And I spend most of my time on a ranch, with only my nieces for company.

And, he wished he could say, as he lifted his large hand to knock on the leaded-glass door, *I don't want a wife, Miss Bliss. I want a lover.*

2

"WHY HASN'T A MAN LIKE you found a wife yet, Owen?"

Suzanne leaned forward in her chair to see who Ella—or was it Louisa?—was greeting at their front door. She expected an older, more mature man to enter the room. The ladies had explained that a man was coming for their expertise and matchmaking advice. "The poor man has *responsibilities*," Louisa had explained, stressing the last word.

"It's not an ordinary situation," Ella conceded. "But then, we've always enjoyed a challenge, haven't we, Louisa?"

And then the knock on the door and Ella's excitement at greeting her guest left Suzanne waiting curiously for the potential groom. She couldn't wait to hear what the problem was with "the poor man" and his extraordinary situation. Too old, too young, too hairy, too bald...or did he stutter or lisp or spit when he spoke?

Suzanne certainly didn't expect a tall rancher in a buckskin coat to walk into the Victorian living room with a baby in his arms. She remembered to close her mouth just in time to be introduced to the second-largest man she'd ever met. The first played defensive end for the New England Patriots and constantly referred to her as "Su-zoo-baby."

The visitor didn't attempt to answer the woman's nosy question, but he did remove his Stetson after he entered the living room. Suzanne saw brown hair, dark eyes, a square, clean-shaven face and an expression that looked more resigned than aggravated with the Bliss lady's personal question. He looked to be about thirty, she guessed, but with some men it was hard to tell.

"Owen, come meet our guest," the tall Bliss sister said, leading the man to where Suzanne perched on an ornate velvet sofa. "Miss Suzanne Greenway. From New York. She's here to do a story on the festival for her magazine. Miss Greenway, this is Owen Chase. He will be a good bachelor for you to feature in your article."

"Hello," she said to the cowboy giant, but the man's attention was taken as the baby grabbed for the brim of his hat.

"My, how that little girl has grown," exclaimed the shorter, rounder sister as she hurried to keep up.

Suzanne stood, though she didn't know why. Maybe it was the only way she could see the man without breaking her neck. The baby—the beautiful, red-cheeked baby—smiled at her and held out her arms. Suzanne took her without thinking if she should or not. And the man let her tumble into Suzanne's arms. She was a handful, a sweet-smelling child whose pink snowsuit and matching blanket felt cool to the touch.

"She's not shy of strangers, I see," Ella said, giving Suzanne a sharp look. "Do you have children, Miss Greenway?"

"No. Only nieces and nephews." The baby reached for Suzanne's hair and caught some curls in her fist.

"Melanie," the man said, his voice low and a little hoarse. "Be careful."

"She's fine," Suzanne assured him as the baby tugged on her hair. She sat down and settled the child in her lap, automatically unzipping the little snowsuit and rearranging the blanket so the child wouldn't overheat. She realized too late she wouldn't be able to take notes as long as she held the baby. "I'm used to it."

The skinny Miss Bliss sat down on the sofa next to her. "You're not engaged to be married, are you?"

"No." Not anymore.

"Are you seeing someone special?"

"No."

"Ah," Ella—at least Suzanne thought her name

was Ella—said, sounding pleased. "That means you may find a husband while you're here."

"I really don't want a husband, Miss Bliss."

"Ah," she said again. "You may change your mind after meeting some of our—"

"Ella," the other sister snapped. "Do stop for a moment. Miss Greenway is here on business, remember?" She gestured toward a large wing chair. "Sit down in that chair over there, Owen. It should hold you. Would you like some tea? It's not a bad blend, for an Earl Grey, but I prefer the jasmine."

"Well," he said, looking for all the world as if he'd rather be anyplace else on earth. In the middle of a blizzard with his cattle, perhaps, Suzanne thought. Or trying to stop a stampede. "I shouldn't—"

"Stay long?" Ella finished for him. "Of course you should. You're on the top of the list this year, along with Calder, but we're not counting him right now because he's not in town. So there is much to discuss."

"The top of the list," he repeated, managing to sit down in the chair without breaking it. "That's what I was afraid of."

"And Miss Greenway needs a bachelor," Louisa explained, pouring a cup of tea. She set it on the mahogany table at the man's elbow.

"For my story." Suzanne wished he would look at her. She wondered if he thought this was as humorous as she did. *Miss Greenway needs a bachelor.* "I'd like to use a personal angle by following one person throughout the festival as he—or she—searches for, um, a spouse. The ladies suggested that you might be the perfect candidate."

"I doubt that," he rumbled, but his gaze was on the baby, whose palm patted Suzanne's chin.

He would photograph well, she decided. He was all-male, with that rough Western look that appealed to some women. Okay, she amended, noting the attractive lines around his eyes. The look appealed to females of all ages, and this particular bachelor— with his gorgeous baby—would make a better focus for the story than some cocky twenty-one-year-old with a beer in his hand. Maybe her story would make the cover, especially if it included the future Mrs. Chase, courtesy of the town's matchmakers.

"You don't want to get married?" Suzanne asked. She wondered if his wife had died. Or run off. Or if he'd never married the mother of the child, but for some strange reason wound up with custody of their daughter.

He looked at her then, looked at her for a long moment before he spoke. Suzanne saw the intelligence in the dark eyes that held her own with his gaze. He sighed, appearing for all the world as if his patience was about to expire. "I admit I need some help raising my nieces," he stated, in that low voice of his.

Suzanne held her breath. For some unknown and ridiculous reason she waited for him to continue. Nieces, he'd said. Plural. There were more.

"But..." He frowned. His attention once again went to the baby, who squirmed on Suzanne's lap and attempted to get down.

"But?" Suzanne turned the child to face Ella Bliss, who clapped her hands to divert the baby's attention, and then looked at the large rancher.

"But?" Louisa urged from her chair beside her sister.

"I don't have time to date, Miss Louisa," he said. "And even if I did, not many women want a ready-made family."

"They don't?" Ella frowned. "That's ridiculous, Owen. Any woman would be proud to raise such fine girls. They're *Chases*, after all, which is nothing to sneeze at."

"Chases?" Suzanne let the child crawl across the maroon velvet cushion to visit the woman.

"Original settlers," Ella explained, letting the child examine the thick buttons on her cardigan sweater. "One of the oldest families in the county."

"And lately, one of the unluckiest," Louisa added, sighing. Owen said nothing, but he looked at the fragile teacup near him as if debating whether to attempt picking it up.

The man had the largest hands she'd ever seen, so

Suzanne watched, fascinated, as the rancher managed to grip the delicate handle between his finger and his thumb. He took a sip, then set it down again as carefully as he'd picked it up. "Thanks for the drink, ladies, but Mel and I need to get going."

"So soon?" Ella reached out and touched his arm. "We haven't discussed your requirements."

"The Wish List," Louisa explained to Suzanne. "It helps Ella get a sense of what the young men look for in a woman."

Suzanne reached for her notepad and pen, then waited for Owen Chase to announce his preferences.

He frowned. "You're going to write this down?"

"Yes, if you don't mind."

"I mind," he said, "even though there isn't any list. There aren't any women. And there won't be any potential brides to meet during the festival."

"Why not?"

"Oh, Owen," Louisa sighed. She reached out and patted his jean-clad knee. "Don't be shy. Just tell Ella the kind of woman you're looking for."

"Yes, dear," her sister agreed. "We'll take it from there. All you have to do is show up at the potluck."

"When is that?" Suzanne asked.

"Tomorrow. It's on the brochure I gave you."

She riffled through her notes and found the gold-edged sheet that listed the events, times and locations. "You're very organized."

"We've had years to perfect it," Ella said. "Our ancestor, Horace Bliss, brought the first wagonload of mail-order brides to the town. The matches were amazingly successful."

"There were fifty men to every woman, you see," Louisa added. "The men felt very fortunate."

"I'm sure they did." Suzanne tried not to laugh. She pictured hundreds of excited Montana bachelors surrounding a wagonful of women. "How did the women choose who they would marry?"

"The men chose," Owen said, rising from his chair. He stepped past Suzanne and lifted the baby from the Bliss sofa before she could tumble to the floor. "Or so the story goes."

"Yes, well, never mind that." Ella waved to the baby. "She's a dear little girl. Any woman would be lucky to be her mother, don't you think so, Suzanne?"

Suzanne almost said yes, but caught herself just in time. Motherhood and marriage and Melanie were none of her business. The blatant matchmaking attempt could be ignored—or included in her article.

"We should be going," he said. The baby giggled and wrapped her arms around his neck. "Darcy's at school waiting for a ride home." He glanced toward Suzanne, his expression surprisingly kind. "It was nice meeting you. I hope you enjoy Bliss."

"Thanks," she said, strangely unwilling to let this man walk away. "I'll be in touch."

He paused. "Why?"

"You're my bachelor," she said. "For my magazine."

Owen Chase frowned. "I don't—"

"You're perfect," she said, hoping to forestall any objections he might want to make. "Readers would love to know what happens to you during the festival."

"I doubt that," he replied, but he almost smiled. "I think your magazine can do better."

"Nonsense." Ella blocked his path to the door. "If you don't give us a list, Owen, we must produce our own on your behalf." Her eyes narrowed as she proceeded to tick off the wifely assets needed for Owen's future spouse. "Domestic, maternal and patient. She mustn't mind living on a ranch and dealing with animals."

"Good horsemanship," Louisa added. "And she should be able to drive a truck."

"Owen can teach her those things later," Ella said, seeming oblivious to the man's loud sigh. Suzanne wondered how much longer his patience would last. The baby fidgeted in his arms and kicked his thighs as she stretched upward to grab his hat. He didn't seem to notice.

"Ladies," he said. "Thanks for the tea. Good luck with the festival."

"We'll see you tomorrow at the potluck supper?"

He hesitated. "Yeah, for a little while. And then—"

"And the dance?" Ella asked.

"Maybe." He moved forward, and Ella stepped back to let him reach the front door. He opened it, but paused halfway through to look back at the women. "You forgot something on that list, Miss Ella," he said, looking so serious that Suzanne knew he was teasing.

"Really?" The elderly lady appeared intrigued. "Tell us and we'll do our best, dear."

He glanced toward Suzanne with a slight smile that made him look almost handsome. "Well, ladies, I'm partial to redheads." With that, he was out the door. As Ella closed it behind him they heard his boots thudding down the front steps.

"My, my," Ella murmured, turning to Suzanne. "Did you hear that? He liked your red hair."

"It's not exactly red," she said. "More like blond with red highlights and—"

"I swear," Louisa announced, patting Suzanne's arm. "Owen Chase flirted with you. How lovely!"

"Owen Chase doesn't flirt." Ella eyed Suzanne's hair once again. "Strawberry blond," she said.

"That's what we used to call that shade of red. *He's* your bachelor, Miss Greenway."

"Suzanne," she said. "Please call me Suzanne. And I don't think Mr. Chase wanted to be in my article. He seemed like a very private man."

"You'll convince him otherwise," Ella assured her, taking her elbow and steering her toward the couch. "I have an excellent feeling about this."

"He flirted," her sister repeated, following them into the living room. "He was charming. Much like Robert used to flirt, remember, Ella?"

Ella ignored her. She handed Suzanne her notebook. "You'll go to the potluck supper, of course, but there's much to do before then."

"Who's Robert?" Suzanne glanced toward Louisa.

"A former beau." Louisa blushed.

"Not exactly a beau," Ella replied, though her sister looked as if she wanted to argue. "Now, let's talk about the festival and how we intend to find wives for our most eligible men. We'll start," she said, smiling a little as she studied Suzanne, "with Owen, of course. He might be easier than we thought."

Surely the elderly women didn't think that they could find a wife for the man. And they couldn't think that Suzanne would be a candidate. She tried not to laugh aloud, but she sat on the couch and faced Ella.

"Okay," she said, picking up her pen. "Tell me about the cowboy."

HE'D BEEN AN IDIOT. He'd stared at her. He'd said nothing, except for that stupid remark about her hair. *I'm partial to redheads.* What had he been thinking? Oh, he knew exactly what he'd had on his mind. Just looking at the damn woman had made him think of beds and sex and long interrupted nights.

Owen fumbled with the seat belts, but managed to get Mel strapped into her car seat before she complained. The baby grinned at him as if she knew how stupid her uncle felt.

"Don't worry," he told her, adjusting the pink blanket around her head and ears. "You'll be home soon, before Uncle Owen makes a fool of himself in front of any more beautiful women."

And Suzanne was beautiful, he thought, shutting the passenger door and heading around to his side of the truck. That long hair, those long legs encased in fancy slacks, and a perfect figure poured into a green sweater would make any man think the kinds of things he was thinking.

He'd wanted to do a lot more than drink tea and answer questions from the Bliss ladies. And here he had a baby in the truck. And a niece to pick up. Ever since Judy died, he'd been a man of responsibilities and duties.

Those duties included waiting at the school for basketball practice to end, not lusting after some reporter from back East. He parked his truck in the gymnasium parking lot and waited for Darcy.

"Hey." Gabe, bachelor father and neighbor, walked over and motioned for him to roll down his window.

"What are you doing here?" Gabe's kids weren't high-school age.

"School play rehearsal," his friend replied. "Let's hit Sam's for supper," he suggested.

"It's going to be mobbed." Mobbed with potential brides and grooms, a regular lonely hearts club with french fries. "We're not exactly going to fit in."

"Yeah, well..." His friend shrugged. "We can watch the action and remember when we were young."

"Beats cooking." Especially if you had to cook while holding a baby in one arm.

"Anything beats cooking," Gabe replied. "I'll meet you there in a few minutes."

Owen nodded and rolled up his window before Mel breathed in too much cold air. He and Gabe O'Connor were pretty much in the same situation, though Gabe had been alone a lot longer and had more confidence raising kids than Owen could ever dream of. He wondered if Gabe had ever met a woman he couldn't resist—not counting his late wife.

Owen knew that a bachelor had no business lusting after a long-legged redhead who wanted nothing more than to follow him around while he made a fool of himself.

"SHE WANTS TO FOLLOW YOU around," Gabe repeated, twenty minutes later when they were settled in a corner booth at Marryin' Sam's. "And this is a problem?"

"It's for her magazine."

"So?"

"She's beautiful."

"Don't look so miserable." Gabe laughed. "You need a woman, my friend. How long is this beautiful redhead going to be in town?"

"I don't know. Long enough to get some pictures and earn her salary, I guess." He looked over at the table where the kids laughed as they ate hamburgers and fries. Darcy was smiling, which was some kind of miracle considering what the kid had been through this past year. Losing a mother and a stepfather had rocked the kid's world, yet she kept up with her school work and helped with the baby when she could. Melanie slept in the car seat nestled beside him in the booth.

"Tell her you'll help her out, Chase. How bad could it be?"

"She needs a bachelor to follow through the festival. I'd have to talk to women and act like I was interested in getting married. The Bliss sisters set the whole thing up."

Gabe groaned. "Don't tell me they asked you over for tea and told you you're on the top of the list this year."

"Yeah. And I'll bet you're number two."

The rancher winced. "The last thing I want is to get married again."

"You know that and I know that, but Ella and Louisa might have other ideas."

Gabe swore softly and reached for the ketchup. "Not me, pal. You, on the other hand, need a wife." He nodded toward the sleeping baby. "As soon as she starts walking, you're not going to get much work done. I'm amazed you can work at all."

"I'll hire someone when the time comes."

"It's not easy finding help. Not out here. Your best bet is to find some nice lady and get married. Your troubles would be over." He looked at the kids at the nearby table. "It's not easy raising girls."

"I've never been good with women," Owen confessed. It was an understatement.

"Maybe your redhead likes cowboys."

"She's a city girl, through and through."

"But underneath? You never know."

Owen knew, all right. He didn't have a prayer.

"No." Louisa clanked her teacup against its saucer so hard that Ella was surprised the china didn't shatter all over the table. Really, her sister had no business being moody at this time of year.

"Louisa, she's perfect for him. You said yourself he flirted with her. That remark about her red hair—"

"Was simply a remark, Ella. I've had second thoughts."

"Second thoughts about what?"

"About matchmaking. I think..." she said, pausing to take a deep breath. "I think I might retire."

"Retire? From what?"

"Matchmaking. I don't feel, well, enthusiastic enough anymore."

"You seemed enthusiastic enough when Owen was here, when the Greenway woman held that baby like she was born to do so. Why, the color of their hair *matched*. It gave me goose bumps, Lou. And you felt it, too. You had that look on your face. That matchmaking look."

"*If* I did—and I'm not admitting to anything, Ella—*if* I did, it was only briefly. Just a twinge, easily explained by romantic foolishness." She stood, turning her back to her sister while she cleared the tea things and set them on the tray to take to the kitchen.

"What about tomorrow?"

"Tomorrow?" Louisa didn't turn around.

"You know darn well tomorrow we start the festival with a speech about Horace and the town's tradition. It's your turn to announce the winner of the door prize."

"You shall do it for me."

"But tradition—"

"Tradition can go on without me," her sister declared, then bustled out of the room as if she had a million things to do before *Jeopardy* came on. Ella loved that television show. She knew it kept her mind sharp and alert, warding off some of the dangers of old age. And there were a lot of dangers when someone was her age, such as forgetting to take medication. Falling and breaking a hip.

And losing interest in life. Clearly something was wrong with Louisa. She'd never been as accomplished a matchmaker as Ella was, but her sister had good instincts and an abundance of common sense.

This recent display of temper couldn't possibly be anything more than Lou having a bad day. Perhaps she should send out to the drugstore for a laxative.

Or reorder the damn tea.

3

By the time the Bliss ladies finished telling her about
Owen, Suzanne had decided that she never wanted
to see him again. A man who dedicated his life to
raising his dead sister's children while running a
ranch, a man who didn't date—or at least Ella had
never heard of any women in Owen's life—and who
actually wanted to get married and live happily ever
after, well, a man like that was too good to be true.

And incredibly romantic, if Suzanne wanted to
think in those terms. She did, of course, but only for
the magazine. She was through with love, romance
and men. Six months ago, when the man she thought
she loved hadn't bothered to show up for their wedding, Suzanne had invited the wedding guests to
take home chunks of wedding cake. She'd donated
the food to the local homeless shelter and the flowers
to a nursing home.

Her older sisters had done what they could to
comfort her, but Suzanne hadn't wanted to seem too
pathetic. It was bad enough being the youngest of
the family without making a spectacle of herself

when the spotlight was on her. Her sisters gathered up the wedding gifts and comforted the groom's mortified parents. Aunt Nancy and Uncle Ned assured Suzanne they'd always thought Greg wasn't good enough for her, so she was better off without him. Suzanne had agreed, donated her wedding dress to the Salvation Army and her veil to her six-year-old niece. Hey, when something was over, it was over. For good. Forever.

And advertising a broken heart had never been her style.

"Thank you for everything," she'd told the ladies after she'd taken some photographs of them posed in front of the fireplace, ancestor Horace Bliss, the Original Matchmaker, looking down from a painting above the mantel.

She wanted sleep. She wanted to check her e-mail. She wanted to go home and forget all about Bliss, Montana, and its silly traditions and its paragon of virtue, Owen Chase. But most of all—before she found her inn and her laptop—she wanted something to eat. The Western-style restaurant in the center of town looked like the logical choice of eating establishments: it was well lit, on Main Street, and a truck pulled out of a parking spot directly in front, leaving Suzanne plenty of space to park her car.

Suzanne met three men and five women on her way to the front door of the restaurant. A cheerful group, they passed her as they headed down the street toward the movie theater. All five wore bright yellow buttons with Bliss emblazoned against a red heart.

"A charitable donation, ma'am," one young man explained after she'd stopped him to ask. He grinned down at her. "Raises money for the health clinic."

"Does everyone wear one?"

"If they want to," a young woman said. "There's a number on the back for the raffles." She pointed to the café. "You can buy one at any of the stores in town for five dollars."

"Thanks." Suzanne would make a note of that, after eating a hamburger and maybe a piece of apple pie. Marryin' Sam's was the kind of place that looked as if it served apple pie. And she could smell french fries every time the door opened to release customers.

Suzanne headed inside, determined to shake the strange feeling that she had landed in a foreign country. The Bliss sisters had filled her head with history and romantic success stories, with weddings and magic and—most of all—the need to find the perfect woman for Owen Chase.

Who happened to be standing directly in front of her.

"Hi, again," she said, looking up—way up—to meet his gaze. He looked surprised, then frightened, which made Suzanne feel a little bit guilty. He probably thought she was following him around already, hoping he would talk to potential brides and give her a good story. "Don't worry," she said. "I'm not following you around town." He didn't look convinced, so she added, "Really, I'm only here for dinner."

The baby rested her head on the man's wide shoulder, her eyes closed, but Owen smiled. Almost. "The food's good."

"Are you coming or going?" She hated to eat alone, though she doubted this man would be a talkative dinner partner. Still, she wouldn't mind visiting with him. For the article. Not because he had kind eyes and looked like the most gentle man she'd ever seen.

"Going," he said, shifting the baby in his arms as another man herded a group of children toward them. "As soon as my niece...oh, here you are."

"Hi," a pretty, ponytailed teenager said, then looked up at Owen. "You want me to take her?"

"No, she's asleep. Darcy, this is Suzanne Greenway. She's a reporter here in town to do a story. Miss Greenway, meet my other niece, Darcy."

"Hi," Suzanne said, and held out her hand to shake the teenager's. The girl looked to be about thirteen, with auburn hair and dark brown eyes the same shade as her uncle's.

"Hi. What kind of story?"

"I work for *Romantic Living* magazine. Ever heard of it?"

The girl shook her head.

"My boss sent me here to write about the matchmaking festival in the 'most romantic town in the West.'"

"You're kidding, right?" the girl asked, intrigued. "Bliss is too small to be the 'most' anything."

"I'll send you a copy of the article next year and you can decide for yourself," Suzanne promised, then turned back to Owen. "Can we meet sometime tomorrow? You name the time and the place."

"Miss Greenway, I don't—"

"Suzanne," she corrected. "Please."

"Suzanne," he said, his voice low. He looked down at her with a very serious expression. "I don't want my personal life showing up in a magazine article."

"Owen?" A handsome, weathered man stepped away from the counter and stopped next to the rancher. "We're all..." He stopped when he saw Suzanne, and he grinned. "Hello."

"Hi." She held out her hand. "Suzanne Greenway. I'm—"

"Here to do a story," he said, shaking the hand she offered. "I heard. Gabe O'Connor, Owen's friend and neighbor."

"Nice to meet you. Are you one of the town's eligible bachelors, too?"

Owen chuckled, surprising Suzanne with his quick smile. "He is. You should interview him, not me. Ella Bliss is sure to invite him over for tea this week, too."

"Owen's the one who needs a wife," Gabe said. "Help him out, will you, Suzanne?"

"I'll try, but he's stubborn."

Darcy rolled her eyes. "Uncle Owen is always stubborn," she declared. "But he should go out on dates once in a while, so he doesn't get too lonesome."

"That's enough," Owen said, looking decidedly uncomfortable being the center of attention. His gaze dropped to Suzanne's hair, which had come loose from the barrette at the nape of her neck. She reached behind her and made an effort to control it, hoping she looked somewhat professional instead of windblown and sleepy.

"You're not going to let the lady eat alone, are you, Owen?" Gabe winked at Suzanne as two young children hurried up to him. "My kids," he explained. "We have to get home. Darcy has homework and Mel—"

"Is unconscious," his friend interrupted. "I'll take Darcy with me. You can pick her up on your way home. Stay and keep the lady company."

"Go ahead, Uncle Owen," his niece said. "I can do my math at Gabe's house, no problem."

"Well..." Owen looked so uncomfortable that Suzanne felt sorry for him.

"You don't have to," she assured him. "I'm used to eating by myself," she fibbed. "Go put your baby to bed. Maybe we can get together tomorrow, sometime when you're not too busy." She stepped sideways, hoping to allow the men room to move toward the door, but Owen didn't budge.

"No," he said slowly. "I'll stay."

"See you later," his friend said, herding the children out the door. "Take your time." He paused and smiled at Suzanne. "I'm sure we'll meet again. It's a small town."

"It was nice meeting you," she said. He reminded her a little of her oldest brother-in-law, who was a police officer in Boston and a great tease.

"Same here." He turned then, following the children out of the restaurant. A blast of cold air hit Suzanne's neck.

She shivered and turned back to Owen, who still had the baby against his shoulder. She noticed that he carried a car seat in his right hand and had a baby's bottle sticking out of his jacket pocket. She wondered if he knew how charming he looked. "So I've trapped you into an interview," she said. "Or is this off the record?"

"Off the record," he said, motioning toward an empty booth. They waited for the waitress to finish cleaning the table before Owen fiddled with the car seat and set the sleeping baby next to him on the padded bench. "She sleeps anywhere," he said.

"Even amid all this noise?" Suzanne slid into the booth and peered over at the child, who looked for all the world as if she was asleep in a soundproof nursery. "She's beautiful. How do you manage?"

"Her grandmother helped me out at first," he said, and handed Suzanne a menu from behind the ketchup bottle. "Ella and Louisa told you the whole story, I'm sure."

Suzanne took the plastic-coated menu and glanced at the selections. "They had a lot to say," she agreed, unbuttoning her coat. "What's good?"

"Pretty much everything. They make the best fries in town, if you don't mind grease."

"I love grease." She grinned at him. "And please tell me they serve apple pie here."

"They serve apple pie here." Once again there was that hint of a smile, and Suzanne thought she detected a twinkle in his eyes.

"Thank God." She turned back to the menu and eyed the hamburger selections. When the waitress came to take her order, she was ready. Owen ordered coffee after Suzanne gave her order for a burger deluxe and a diet cola.

"Writing makes you hungry," he said.

"It's been a long day. No one feeds you on planes anymore." She leaned back against the padded booth. "You have your hands full," she said. "How do you manage?"

"Off the record?"

"Completely."

He unbuttoned his thick jacket to reveal a wide expanse of flannel shirt. "It's never been easy, but it was better when Doreen—she's the girls' grandmother—was around to help out."

"Where is she now?"

"Out in California with her son. She had to have hip replacement surgery." The waitress deposited their drinks, sending Owen into silence once again.

"And there was no one else to take the girls but you?"

"No. I gave Judy—my sister—my word that I would take care of the girls, but this past month has been pretty damn hard."

A man of his word. How rare these days, Suzanne thought, taking a sip of her drink. "So you're hoping the Bliss sisters will find the perfect woman for you. That's pretty amazing."

"I didn't want to be rude. They're nice old ladies and they believe in what they do. Folks around here don't take them too seriously."

"But the festival—"

"Makes money," he said. "No one can figure out exactly how or why the town has such a low divorce rate, but anyone with a business to run is glad to capitalize on that fact. The Bliss sisters believe it started with Horace, but..." He turned to check on the sleeping baby, then picked up his coffee cup.

"But what?"

"Off the record—we wouldn't want to embarrass Ella and Louisa—the story goes that Horace waylaid a wagon of prostitutes on their way to a gold rush town north of here, near the Idaho border. He wanted to start a respectable town, so he promised the women property if they married, had children and stayed married for ten years. It worked."

"You've got to be kidding."

"No, it's true. We don't go around bragging about it, but—"

"I meant, you can't mean that I can't put that story in my article." She could picture the opening lead: "Ladies of Bliss: fact or fiction?"

"We're a little sensitive about it." Again, he gave that slow smile that made her want to lean forward and learn more about him.

"You really would be great for the article, you know." She was insane to be attracted to this man. She would be insane to be attracted to any man, but a giant with children who lived in the middle of Montana?

"I'm not real crazy about having my personal life in a magazine." He took a sip of his coffee. "And I sure don't want people watching while I make a fool of myself." He waved his free hand toward the crowd of laughing young women that had just spilled into the restaurant. "You think any of them are looking for a man who works eighteen hours a day and is raising two girls? I doubt it."

"There are a lot of women who would find your situation intriguing."

"What kind of women and where are they?" He glanced toward the sleeping child once again, then back to Suzanne. "If you see any this week while you're in town, let me know."

"I will. You'll be at that dinner tomorrow night?"

The waitress set a thick plate with an enormous hamburger, toasted bun and a pile of salted fries in front of her, then handed Owen a slip of paper. "My niece's name and my phone number," the waitress explained. "She's coming in from Billings tomorrow. For the weekend. Divorced."

Owen nodded politely.

"She likes kids," the middle-aged woman said. "Has twin boys, but they don't slow her down any."

"Okay." The rancher gave her a polite nod.

"Just thought you'd want to know. Enjoy your dinner," the woman said before hurrying off.

Suzanne watched Owen tuck the piece of paper

into his shirt pocket. "Looks like you're off to a good start. Now you have someone to call tomorrow."

"Mrs. Salter's niece is barely out of her teens," he said, keeping his voice low.

"You're looking for an older woman?" Suzanne gazed down at the plateful of food. "Wow."

"*That's* what I want," she heard Owen mutter, so she glanced up at him as she reached for the ketchup.

"A burger?"

"A woman to look at me like you're looking at your dinner."

"I can't help it," she said, tucking an extra paper napkin in her lap. "I love food. The Bliss ladies think they can find a few candidates. Why don't you let them? Or take the waitress up on her offer to meet her niece?"

He sighed. "I wish they'd leave me alone. Or..." Owen hesitated, clearly uncomfortable with the conversation.

"Or?" Suzanne prompted, helping herself to a thick french fry.

"Find the perfect woman, drop her off at the ranch, and that would be that."

"No muss, no fuss."

"Right."

"Like the good old days, when a man could pick a woman out of a wagon and take her home to the cabin, toss her into bed, then expect her to start cookin' up the vittles." She took a big bite of the burger and decided she would eat lunch here tomorrow, too.

"You're teasing me again."

She nodded, her mouth full.

"Do you *like* dating?" Owen leaned forward. Suzanne shrugged and chewed faster. "You really like going out with some guy you barely know who takes you out to dinner, talks about his job, his favorite football team, and then tries to get you into bed before midnight?"

Suzanne swallowed. "Sometimes it's not that bad." With Greg it hadn't been like that. "Sometimes it's wonderful and romantic and perfect." Until the wedding.

Owen didn't look convinced. He frowned at her and then finished the rest of his coffee, which prompted the waitress to reappear.

"Sometimes," Suzanne continued, "it's even fun."

"Fun." He sighed. "When you're a bachelor in Bliss, this time of year isn't fun."

"Everyone else looks like they're having a good time. People around here seem to be having fun with the whole matchmaking idea."

"What about you? Did you come to Bliss to find a husband?"

"I've no interest in marriage."

Once again Owen gave her that half smile that was too damn charming. "No cookin' up the vittles?" he asked.

"No." She finished her hamburger, and Owen sipped his coffee as if they ate together every night.

"I'd better get going," the man said.

"Thanks for the company. Are you sure you won't change your mind?"

"About what?" He tossed a ten-dollar bill on the table and scooped the child into his arms.

"The article."

Those dark eyes met hers briefly. "You can do anything you please, Miss Greenway. But following *me* around is a waste of time."

He was right, she decided. Tomorrow she would ask the Bliss ladies to recommend another bachelor. She didn't know what it was about this man, but he made her want to curl up under a quilt and make babies.

"HONEY, DO YOU LIKE older men?"

Suzanne eyed the elderly man who held the restaurant door open for her. Owen and his sleeping baby had left, but she'd stayed to ask the cashier for a piece of apple pie to take with her.

"You're letting the cold air in, Pete!"

The oldest cowboy on the planet ignored the waitress's complaint. "I'm serious, honey. I've dreamed of redheads my whole life."

"Thank you, but I'm not here to—"

"He's worth millions," the plump cashier called. "Harmless and all that, but he's a real pain in the you-know-where, Red, so be careful."

Suzanne couldn't help laughing at the man's crest-fallen expression. Or the cashier calling her "Red."

"It was nice meeting you," she said, stepping out into the cold. "Maybe I can interview you for my article."

"Interview?" He followed her outside, his Stetson jammed tight on his head against the wind. "Like for TV? Are you from *Access Hollywood* or somethin'?"

"I'm doing a story for *Romantic Living* magazine," she began to explain, but she started to shiver while digging out the car keys from her coat pocket.

"Romantic living? Honey, I'm your man," he said, tipping his hat. "Pete Peterson, at your service. Call anytime. I'm in the book. I have three sons, but they're pretty much worthless."

"I'll call if I need you," she promised, then unlocked the car and set her little box with its slice of apple pie on the passenger seat.

"I'm not averse to havin' more kids," he called as she got into her car.

She waved goodbye and shut the door against the cold and the sound of the old man's voice. The people around here were a little odd, but definitely entertaining.

GABE OFFERED OWEN a cup of coffee while Darcy complained that he had come to pick her up too soon. The girls had been painting their nails, Gabe explained. The small television on the kitchen counter was tuned to a pro football game, and Gabe looked like he was in the middle of baking a cake. The small kitchen was, as usual, crowded with books, dishes, coats, papers and assorted cans of food that hadn't been put in the cupboards yet. It looked very similar to Owen's own kitchen, except his was bigger and there was more space for clutter.

"We can't leave yet because I can't put my gloves on till my nails are dry," Darcy said, before running back up the stairs when Gabe's daughter called her name. Owen wondered how he'd ever understand teenage girls and if he was a fool to try.

"How'd it go with the redhead?"

Owen took a seat at the kitchen table, where wide-eyed Melanie rested in her car seat. She'd woken when he'd put her in the truck, and had babbled all the way out to Gabe's ranch. At the moment she looked as if she was content, so Owen sipped his coffee and considered his friend's question. "Not bad."

"You want to be more specific?" He picked up a box of cake mix and frowned at the directions.

"Not really. There isn't much to say." Except she had blue eyes that looked at him in a way that made him want to haul her to his bedroom for two or three years. "You want to tell me what you're doing?"

"Baking cupcakes. Joe forgot to tell me he'd volunteered to bring cupcakes for some reading party they're having at school tomorrow." Gabe dumped the contents of the box into a white mixing bowl.

"Call Ella Bliss. You need help more than I do," Owen commented, watching an egg roll off the counter and splatter on the floor. He reached for the roll of paper towels on the table and leaned over to wipe up the mess.

"Thanks," Gabe said, as Melanie began to wail for something to eat. "You're in as much trouble as I am. We need wives, all right, but who'd have us?"

Owen sighed and reached for his niece. He knew who wouldn't have him: a strawberry blonde with a craving for french fries.

4

"UNCLE OWEN, are you going to see her again?"

"Who?"

"The writer with the beautiful hair." Darcy put her empty cereal bowl in the dishwasher and grabbed her ski jacket, backpack and bike helmet.

"Probably."

Darcy paused halfway out the back door and turned to stare at her uncle. "You *are?*"

"What's the problem?"

His niece rolled her eyes. Unfortunately, she did that a lot. "She's not exactly your type."

"My type," he repeated, picking up his coffee cup. "And what would that be?"

"Someone like Mrs. Moore."

"Maggie Moore is a good friend and that's all." And Maggie, childhood friend and now widowed, would always belong—rightfully—to someone else.

Darcy sighed. "You don't have to get married to some stranger just because of me and Mel, you know."

"And you don't have to worry," he said. "I'm not

exactly surrounded by women who want to come home with me, honey." He hoped that would make her smile, but it didn't.

"And if you were? We wouldn't have to move into town, would we?"

"No one's going anywhere. And the only reason I said I was seeing Suzanne Greenway is because she'll be at the potluck supper tonight," he said, hoping he sounded as if he didn't care if he saw the woman or not. The truth was he'd spent a sleepless night thinking about Suzanne and wondering what all that curling hair would feel like cascading over his naked body.

It was not a fantasy that made him particularly proud of himself, but, hell, he was a man. A man who hadn't had sex with a woman in two years, not since he and Lila Mae Ralston had had too much to drink at her going-away party. Lila Mae, a pleasant enough woman, had returned to North Dakota, and Owen had returned to celibacy, only because he'd been too busy out on the ranch to party in town and because drunken sex was not his style.

Though right about now, after a sleepless night, he figured he almost regretted having principles.

"Okay. You won't forget to pick me up at nine-thirty?"

"Nine-thirty?"

"The basketball team is washing dishes tonight at

the hall, remember?" Darcy looked at him as if he had three heads and no brain.

"I remember, honey." He went to the door and tweaked her ponytail. "Be careful on that bike."

"I always am." She gave him a quick kiss and then she was gone. A few minutes later he heard the engine of her motorbike start up. She'd ride the mile and a half to the road and leave the bike for him to retrieve later, since he usually picked her up in town after basketball practice.

Owen grabbed his coat and went upstairs to get the baby. He'd finally met the perfect woman and— just his bad luck—he wasn't free to pursue her.

"IT'S GOING TO BE a fine day, Louisa." Ella bustled into the dining room and ignored her sister's sad face. Louisa didn't look at all enthused about the sunshine breaking through the clouds this morning. There would be no snowstorm to mar the attendance at the supper tonight.

And the supper was where the Bliss ladies made their annual speech.

Ella loved the annual speech. She had tonight's notes in her hand, something to read and reread over breakfast and her second cup of coffee. "I have the speech all written," she said, waving the papers in front of her.

Louisa didn't look the least impressed. "I told you,

Ella, I don't think I'm in the matchmaking mood this year."

"Nonsense." She sat in her usual place, directly across from Louisa, with a view of the street from the east window. "Haven't you perked up yet?"

"I've retired."

"With Suzanne Greenway in town? How could you?" Ella eyed the sidewalk, but there wasn't much to see at seven. The school bus would be along soon, which was always interesting. She wasn't interested in the children, but old man Cameron was certain to back that old Buick of his into that bus one of these mornings, and Ella didn't want to miss it. The foolish old goat had no business driving in the first place, and he insisted on backing out into the street as if his eyes and his brain still worked. Ella had heard that the bus driver herself had a bet with the sheriff that there'd be a crash one day.

"It will never work, Ella. The woman isn't staying long enough to see what a fine young man he is."

Ella defended her choice. "She's smart enough, that one is. And maternal, too. You saw her face when she held the child." Wistful, that's what Ella would call it, but Louisa didn't seem interested. "And I heard they were together at Sam's last night for dinner. Missy saw them and called last night after you went to bed."

Louisa shrugged. "A coincidence, surely."

"You said he flirted with her."

"That doesn't mean they should marry. It means he liked her hair color. I do hope it's natural."

"I'm sure it is," Ella said, hoping that if it wasn't Suzanne wouldn't let anyone know differently.

Louisa stood and smoothed her housecoat. "I should dress," she mused. "And maybe take a walk."

"Well, take your ski pole and don't go near Cameron's driveway, Lou. He's as blind as a bat. He wouldn't see you if you were hanging on to his windshield."

"He noticed me once," Louisa said, lifting her chin in the air the way she did when she wanted to argue. "Father wouldn't let him come calling."

Ella chuckled. "I remember. Father gave him quite a set down."

"There were others, too, but Father said they weren't good enough for a Bliss." Louisa went to the window. "Now look at us, two old ladies living alone and giving speeches on matchmaking. All we need is a dozen or so cats and some lace doilies and we'd be the perfect old lady spinsters."

"I can't imagine marriage," Ella said, picking up her speech once again. "Never could abide the thought of living with a man day in and day out. They're noisy creatures, you know."

"We could use a little noise around here," Louisa retorted.

"Turn the television on, then. The news will give you all the noise you need." Ella studied the first page of her notes. Once again she'd attempted to gain the diners' attention with her opening sentence. She took a sip of her coffee and didn't notice the lukewarm temperature. She'd reread two pages before she looked up and saw Cameron back his battered automobile into the mailbox.

"TRADITION," Ella Bliss announced, her voice booming from the speakers placed around the American Legion Hall, "is everything."

Suzanne wrote that down in her notebook while the crowd of townspeople and visitors held paper cups of punch and waited for the announcement that the buffet was open. The noise of food preparation from the kitchen would have drowned out Ella's words if she hadn't used a microphone; however, nothing could stop the smell of roasting turkey from wafting through the hall.

"The matchmakers of Bliss have brought happiness and joy to hundreds—if not thousands—of men and women in the past 137 years, since Horace Bliss delivered brides to the hardworking men anxious to settle the West."

"And anxious to get their hands on a woman,"

someone said within Suzanne's hearing, much to his friend's amusement.

"And settle the West they did," Ella continued, giving the history of the town and its tradition of happily married couples as if no one had ever heard it before. Suzanne couldn't help but be fascinated. Of course, she knew that it was impossible for one town to actually have the secret to living happily ever after, but as Ella introduced various couples as examples of marital bliss from five decades, Suzanne's reservations faded. Maybe there was something to this, after all....

"So on behalf of my sister and myself, welcome to Bliss and enjoy the supper. Your donations to the raffles go to the library book fund tonight. You can also purchase buttons for the grand prize, a vintage "wedding ring" quilt, at any of our many fine stores in town. Those funds benefit the local health clinic." Ella acknowledged the applause. "Now, Reverend Smith will share a blessing with us, and I invite you to enjoy your meal and spend the evening meeting each other."

Owen slipped into the chair beside Suzanne as the Reverend blessed the gathering and its purpose.

"How are you?" he asked, keeping his voice low. "Are you married yet?"

"No," she said, turning toward him. "Are you?"

"Not quite, but Mrs. Salter—the waitress from last

night—and her niece have cornered me twice at the cheese and crackers table."

"And was the niece pretty?" He wore a neatly pressed, brown-checked shirt and dark slacks, as if tonight mattered. As if he intended to meet someone special at the matchmaking supper. Suzanne suppressed a twinge of envy.

"I'm sure she would be without the purple streak in her hair and the tattoo on her shoulder." He grimaced. "You don't have any tattoos, do you?"

"Dozens." Suzanne closed her notebook and clipped her pen to it. "To keep potential husbands away, of course."

He eyed the crowd of people talking and laughing around the table, one of many banquet tables that filled the hall. "I don't think it's going to work. There are too many men here who look like they wouldn't mind talking to you."

"A few have tried," she told him. "But I told them I was only here to work and they went away."

"They'll be back," Owen assured her. "The minute you put that notebook down and pick up a plate for supper you'll be surrounded."

"Where's the baby tonight?"

"With Louisa Bliss," he said. "She offered to take care of Mel for a couple of hours."

"I wondered why I hadn't seen her." Suzanne

smiled at him. "I guess she'd rather baby-sit for the number one bachelor on the list, huh?"

"She said she didn't feel like matchmaking tonight, so here I am."

"I thought you'd try to avoid me." Suzanne held up her notebook. "Does this mean you're ready to give me an official interview, Mr. Chase?"

"No, thanks. I'm only here because I promised—"

"Hi, Owen," a pretty blond woman cooed, putting her hands on Owen's shoulders as she came up behind his chair. "What are you doing out tonight?"

"Same as you are, Callie," he said, obviously recognizing her voice. She leaned over and a length of silvery hair brushed his cheek.

"Looking for love?" she teased.

He ignored the question. "Supporting a good cause—donating money to the library."

Suzanne wondered if Callie was going to climb over the chair into Owen's lap. Suzanne had brought her camera tonight, but she didn't think she'd take a picture of Owen making a fool of himself with Cowgirl Callie.

"I hear you're looking for a little mother for your nieces," Callie said, stepping around the chair and seating herself in the one next to Owen. She smiled at Suzanne. "Hi. You're the reporter, I'll bet."

"Suzanne Greenway. Nice to meet you."

"I'm Callie—short for 'Calamity'—Whitlow." The

blonde smiled, then scooted her chair closer to Owen's.

"Calamity is an unusual name."

"Nickname," the woman said. "I used to get in a lot of trouble when I was a kid."

She looked only about twenty now, Suzanne thought. "And you're here for the festival?"

"I live here," she explained. "But I'm not married yet, despite whatever my grandmother and her friends have in mind for me."

"What does your grandmother have planned for you?" Calamity wasn't the maternal type, Suzanne figured, and no match for Owen Chase, although he didn't seem the least reluctant to visit with the girl.

"I'm afraid to ask her for the details—oops, there she is. Owen, save a dance for me tomorrow night. It will thrill Granny no end." She hopped off the chair and disappeared into the group of people waiting in line at the serving table.

"Not exactly matronly, is she?"

Suzanne laughed. "No, but she seems to like you."

"I've known her for years. She's not exactly what she seems." He scraped back his chair and stood. "Do you want to get something to eat?"

"You're going to let me watch you look for the future Mrs. Chase?" Suzanne pushed her chair back and tucked the notebook and camera into her oversize shoulder bag.

"I'm not making a fool of myself for any magazine article," he insisted. "And if I wanted to get married, I would have done it before now."

"So, why haven't you?" She slung her bag over her shoulder and followed him through the crowd to the end of the line.

He shrugged. "The right woman never came along, I guess. But I never pictured myself as living alone for the rest of my life, either."

"So you've become willing to let the town's matchmakers work their magic?"

"Well," he said, "I might. Look around. You see lots of happy couples here tonight."

He had a point, she supposed. And there was an almost wistful expression in his dark eyes that made her want to wrap her arms around him and take him home with her. And then she got a grip.

"What about you?" He moved forward and handed her an empty plate. "Anyone ever make you want to get married?"

"Just once."

"And?" he prompted. "Then what?"

"He came, he left, end of story." No, she was not going to fall under the spell of romantic love again, especially not with a lonely rancher. She only had to remember her wedding—what there'd been of it—to get a grip on reality.

Suzanne stood on her tiptoes to see what kind of

food was arranged on the buffet. "Boy, that turkey sure smells good."

"I TRIED," OWEN TOLD GABE. Three awkward conversations with three perfectly nice single women had dwindled into silence when he didn't attempt to ask any of them out. "When it came down to asking for a date, I froze."

"You really are out of practice," his friend said.

"Or just not interested."

"Check out Callie."

The men watched the amply endowed blonde torture three young cowboys over by the punch bowl.

"Too young. And too wild."

"The new woman in town, over there." Gabe pointed to the dessert table. "The one who makes the fancy desserts and coffee on Main Street. Why don't you go after her?"

Owen shrugged. "Not my type. What about you?"

"Seems nice enough, but I can't picture her living on a ranch."

"Yeah," Owen said. "I know what you mean. What are you doing here? Looking for a wife, after all?"

"Hell, no. The kids are at my mother's, so I thought I'd come by here and see how you were doing with the women."

"There are plenty of 'em," he stated. "But I get the feeling I'd be better off staying home this weekend."

"You'll never get any action that way, Chase."

"I'm out of practice with that, too," he said, watching Suzanne interview a middle-aged couple. They introduced a younger man, one of those idiot Lackland brothers, to her. Whichever Lackland it was looked entirely too pleased with himself, as if he had the redhead's clothes off already. Owen didn't like the looks of the kid. When another young man joined the conversation, Owen frowned even harder. Two Lacklands were even worse, especially when they were together. Those boys had a reputation for mauling anything that moved in front of them.

"She can take care of herself," Gabe murmured.

"I doubt it."

"You don't know her at all. It's that red hair's got you tangled up in knots."

"In my dreams that hair is...never mind." Owen made himself take a deep breath, but he didn't take his gaze off the woman at the other side of the room.

"Take her home, then," Gabe said. "Get it out of your system."

"With my teenage niece in the other room? And a baby to feed at 4:00 a.m.? Not likely."

"She must have a room in town."

Owen briefly closed his eyes. Lust made him dizzy.

"You may as well give it your best shot," his friend advised. "Or die trying."

"She's not interested in me," he said. "Except for her story. She wanted to follow me around and see how my search for a wife went."

"So, say yes and pretend you're searching."

"I thought about that. We ate dinner together earlier."

"And?"

"Seven different men came up to the table and asked for her name and number." Owen had almost choked on the cranberry sauce when old Pete Peterson claimed he'd seen her first and asked if she'd had enough time to consider his proposal.

"Good thing Calder isn't in town," Gabe pointed out. "He'd have a hell of a good time watching you suffer."

Calder Brown, the wealthiest and wildest rancher of the three old friends, loved women, whiskey, horses and his freedom. But he was superstitious when it came to the festival, claiming the Bliss ladies should be avoided if a man wanted to stay happy and single and in charge of his own fate. And Calder believed a man's fate lay in bedding any woman who smiled at him and broadcast her availability.

"He left town three days ago, insisting he had to go buy cattle. We should give him a call and tell him what a coward he is."

"Won't do any good. I think he's in Vegas."

Owen envied him. If Owen was in Las Vegas he wouldn't have to see that the younger Lackland had moved too close to Suzanne. In fact, he'd put his arm around her shoulder. He'd *touched* her, for Pete's sake. "Did you see that?"

"She's fine. She moved out of his reach." Gabe gave Owen a push. "Go claim your woman, Chase, if you want her that badly."

He gulped. "I do."

"Then offer to take her home."

"I've got to pick up the baby from Louisa Bliss, and Darcy's in the kitchen waiting for a ride home." He turned to his friend. "There's no way."

"Basketball's your solution." Gabe grinned. "Isn't the team going to Jasper for some kind of weekend round robin?"

"That's not until the weekend after this one. I don't think I have that much time."

"Invite her out to the ranch, and Darcy can spend the night at my place. The baby will sleep or be cute—either way she's bound to charm your red-head."

"If she's still in town."

"Give her a story and she will be," his friend declared. "Women love this town and they love all this damn matchmaking business. She's not going to leave Bliss easily, and besides, she's begging to follow you around. How many women do you have asking to do that, Chase?"

He smiled. "None."

"You're a fool, you know."

"Yeah. But I don't see you going out with anyone, either." And Owen was pretty sure he knew why, but he wouldn't bring up Maggie's name unless Gabe did. And Gabe never did. "Damn, there goes Lackland again." He moved forward, determined to rescue Suzanne from the oversexed twins.

"Try not to spill any blood," Gabe said behind him.

SUZANNE SAW OWEN COMING through the thinning crowd and hoped he would stop and say goodbye before he left the hall. She would have liked one more chance to ask for an interview and his help with her assignment, but she wasn't going to again. The Lackland twins had offered their assistance and they did have a certain boyish charm, even if they were nowhere as appealing as Owen and his motherless baby.

No, she'd given up on Owen, but she hoped he'd talk to her, just, well, because he was one of the few people here in town she felt as if she knew. There was something about the man that made her wish she lived in town and drove a truck and knew the way out to his ranch.

He stopped directly in front of her and gave the young cowboys a look that made them back up a step, then he turned to Suzanne. "I thought you might need a ride home," he said. "Unless you drove?"

"I walked. The place where I'm staying is only a couple of blocks away, but I wouldn't mind a ride."

Owen took her elbow and tried to lead her away from the young men, who had entertained her with rodeo stories. "Come on, then. It's getting late."

Suzanne dug in her heels. "Wait a second. It's only nine o'clock and I have to get a picture of Joe and Jimmy Lackland here."

"Were they bothering you?"

"Who?"

"These idiot Lacklands."

"No, of course not." She dug her camera from her shoulder bag and turned toward the twins. "Okay, fellas, give me a big smile." They grinned, and she adjusted the focus and then clicked the shutter. The boys blinked against the flash and Suzanne thanked them once more. They tipped their hats, eyed Owen and then hurried off. She turned to the rancher. "You scared them away."

"Why would I do that?"

"I have no idea, but I do think they were afraid of you."

He smiled, obviously pleased with himself. "Where are you staying? The Marry-Me-Motel or Blissful Nights Bed and Breakfast?"

"Blissful Nights," she said. "There's really a Marry-Me-Motel?"

"Absolutely," he said, taking her arm once again. "And then there's Cinderella's, a place where you can rent a wedding dress."

"I went in there today. They had quite a selection." And they sold wedding cake toppers, little ceramic cowboy grooms and brides who wore boots. It had taken every ounce of self-control she had not to buy one.

"There's a bar outside of town called Wedding Bell Blues. They put on pretty good wedding parties—nothing fancy, and everyone wears their best Levi's."

"Bliss takes this wedding business seriously."

"It's not just the festival," Owen explained. "Lots of people come here to get married or on their honeymoon, just to say they did. For good luck. The mayor's favorite line is 'Bliss is our business.'"

She would write that down the minute she arrived back in her room. It would make a great caption underneath one of the photos of the stores lining Main Street.

"Where's your coat?" he asked.

"Over there by yours, where we had dinner." It didn't take them long to retrieve the coats or to bundle up against the cold. Most of the people had gone home, except for a few groups who were still deep in conversation. "I wonder how much money was raised tonight."

"You can ask Ella in the morning. She knows everything," he said, helping her with her coat. His large hands brushed her shoulders, making her shiver. She lifted her hair over the collar and tugged on her thick knitted hat and gloves.

"Just a minute," Owen said, as they passed the kitchen. He opened the door and called to his niece, "Darcy, I'll be back in fifteen minutes. Will you be done by then?" She must have agreed, because Owen nodded and turned toward Suzanne. "The basketball team volunteered to wash dishes tonight."

"Your girls keep you busy."

He didn't argue or agree, but instead led her out the front doors into the cold November night. He touched her arm to guide her to the left, toward the parking area around the side of the brick building. Suzanne hurried to keep up with his long strides, and when they reached his truck, she huddled in her coat while he unlocked the passenger door for her.

"Don't worry," she told him, once they were both

ínside the truck and he had shut his door. "I'm not going to bother you anymore about the article. You're safe."

"Safe?" He turned to her.

"Those nice young men—twins, I think they said—offered to take me to the dance tomorrow with them, and Pete Peterson said he'd give me the senior citizen's tour of Bliss tomorrow anytime I want." She noticed Owen didn't attempt to start the truck. In fact, he continued to frown at her.

"Owen, it's awfully cold in—"

"They are not 'nice young men,'" he interrupted. "And old Pete may look harmless, but he isn't exactly an innocent old man, either." He turned away from her and shoved the key into the ignition. "We'll have heat in a minute."

"I really can take care of myself," she assured him. "I live in New York."

"Right." He put the truck in reverse and backed out of the parking space, then pulled onto Main Street.

Suzanne didn't know what to say. She was touched by his concern, but she knew she could handle just about anything by herself. She'd been taking care of herself since she was eighteen, and very well, too. Of course, having money helped.

"Look," she said, when he pulled in front of the

large white house where she had rented a room. "It's not that I don't appreciate your help."

He didn't turn off the engine, which had just begun to pump welcome warm air through the dashboard vents. "Forget I said anything," he said again.

"I'd rather have you," she explained, wishing he would look at her. She didn't want to hurt this man's feelings. She'd never met anyone like him before. She leaned closer and touched his arm. "I spoke to my editor this morning and told her about you and your nieces. And how the Bliss ladies had a list and you were the name at the top. She was fascinated."

"Say that again." He glanced at her hand on his arm.

"She was fascinated."

Owen shook his head. "No, the first part."

Suzanne smiled at him. "I'd rather have you?"

"That's a dangerous thing to say to a man," he said, drawing closer. "Especially one who's on the top of the Bliss list."

And before she could laugh, he kissed her.

5

OWEN HADN'T PLANNED to kiss her, not until she smiled at him. That smile, combined with the darkness inside the truck, the cold night and his frustration, led him to pull her into his arms and kiss her.

Her lips were warm and very, very soft. Owen sensed her surprise and then she relaxed against his mouth and kissed him back. His fingers tangled in those red curls; his palms held her head gently as his mouth slanted across hers and tasted heaven. Owen could have kissed her 'til midnight, it was that good. Their thick jackets kept their bodies inches apart, but somehow that didn't matter. Yet. It was enough— well, almost enough—to make love to her lips, to feel her gloved hands on his waist and know she was holding him to her instead of pushing him away.

Owen hadn't planned to tease her lips with his tongue, either, but he forgot he was parked on a public street and that he was a man of responsibilities and duties. He was only a man, first of all, and the temptations were too great, especially when Suzanne's lips parted for more and he entered her mouth as slowly and sweetly as if he was making love to her body with the part of him that was much larger than his tongue.

He knew it was dangerous, but Owen stopped thinking the moment Suzanne reached for him instead of the door handle. He hadn't forgotten how to kiss, but he hadn't remembered that trying to make love to a woman in the front seat of a pickup truck was damn near impossible, especially when the truck was running and someone behind them flashed his lights and honked a horn.

That someone was going to pay, Owen decided, seconds after Suzanne pulled away from him. "What the—"

"It's okay," she whispered.

"No—"

"I'd better go." This time she did reach for the handle and, gathering up her large bag in her other hand, opened the door and hopped out.

"Tomorrow," he tried to say before she shut the door and blocked his view of her, but he didn't hear the word come out of his mouth. And then she was gone, up the sidewalk and onto the lighted front porch. He'd wanted to tell her that he'd give her the tour of the county. He'd take her to the damn dance tomorrow. He'd even risk making a fool of himself and dance—if that would make her happy.

Owen Chase didn't want to be a bachelor any

longer, but first he had to find out what the joker behind wanted before he picked up his kids.

"DID YOU ENJOY YOURSELF, dear?"

"Yes, Mrs. Whitlow. Very much," she told her
hostess. The elderly lady met her at the door and
ushered her inside, as if she'd known Suzanne was
about to use the key she'd been given, and intended
to save her the trouble.

"I hope I didn't wake you."

"It's only nine-thirty, dear. I don't go to bed until
late, long after David Letterman and those reruns of
Law and Order. I just love that show." She closed the
heavy door behind Suzanne and followed her to the
stairs. "How did you like our supper? I caught a
glimpse of you early on and you seemed to be having a good time. Did you find a man for your story?"

"Everyone was very helpful," Suzanne said, wanting nothing more than to run up those stairs and sink
into the double bed with its down comforter. She
hoped she didn't look as if she'd just been kissed by
the only man she wanted for "her story." "I got some
great interviews."

"And Owen Chase brought you home. How nice."

"Yes." There were no secrets in Bliss. Had Mrs.
Whitlow been peeking out of her lace-covered windows?

"Did I hear someone honking?"

Suzanne shrugged and decided to change the subject. "I met your granddaughter, Callie."

"Now there's a character for your magazine story," the woman said. "Pay no attention to her nonsense. She's a good girl—or she will be once she settles down."

Suzanne eased toward the stairs. "She's very beautiful."

"She's also hell on wheels," the woman said with a sigh. "Would you like some tea before you go upstairs?"

"I think I'll just go to bed, but thank you."

"Is your room comfortable? It's one of the nicest, I think, though I try to make each room seem special," Mrs. Whitlow said.

"It's lovely," Suzanne assured her.

"Breakfast is served between seven and nine, don't forget, but if you want to sleep late I always leave coffee and pastries in the dining room for the late risers."

"I won't forget. Thank you. Good night."

"Good night!" the lady called behind her. Suzanne hurried up the stairs and turned right on the second floor to the second room on the left. The house, one of those solid Victorian homes that lined the side streets of Bliss, had polished wood floors and tall windows, Oriental rugs and thick velvet drapes. Suzanne's room was papered in shades of celery and yellow, with cream-painted woodwork and dark cherry furniture. Vanilla potpourri sat in a crystal bowl on top of a dresser, and the four-poster bed was topped with a comforter printed with fat yellow roses.

Right now she wanted to bury herself under those roses and remember what it was like to kiss a cowboy. It had been pretty darn exciting, that's what it had been.

Lust usually was.

And there was nothing wrong with lust, unless a woman foolishly decided there was more to it than chemical attraction and spiking hormonal activity and excitement brought on by abstinence. Hers, not his. She didn't know anything about Owen's sex life, but until he'd kissed her she'd assumed he didn't have much of one or the ladies in town wouldn't feel sorry for him and try to marry him off to the first maternally minded woman who could drive a truck through a cow pasture without hitting a fence.

Suzanne put on her nightgown and washed her face and remembered to use moisturizer. But all she could think about was how Owen had kissed her and she'd kissed him back. She really had to wonder if the man hadn't had a lot of practice. He was a deadly kisser, the kind of kisser who could entice a supposedly smart woman to act like an infatuated teenager.

And the kind of man who made a woman forget she had no use for men at all.

"THE LITTLE DEAR SLEPT like an angel," Louisa whispered. She helped Owen bundle up the child before taking her out to the truck for the drive home. "I hate to see her go out in the cold."

"I'll keep her warm," Owen promised, knowing that Darcy would sit in the back seat with the baby and make sure she was comfortable. "Thanks a lot, Louisa, for helping out."

"I loved it," she told him. "I'd be happy to do it again if you like. It can't be easy getting out at night when you have a little one like Melanie to care for."

"It's pretty much impossible," Owen agreed, tucking the baby against his chest. "But I'm not much for going out at night, anyway."

"And there's the problem," Louisa said, following him to the front door. "You have to go *out* in order to find that special lady to bring *home*."

Owen stopped, his hand on the doorknob. "What special lady?"

"No one in particular, Owen," she said. "Unless you have someone in mind?"

"No," he lied, thinking of a little while ago when he'd had Suzanne in his arms. She wasn't the kind of woman a man wanted to leave. "No one at all."

"What about that nice Greenway girl? Have you decided to help her with her magazine story?"

"I'm still thinking about it," he said, trying to open the door without knocking Louisa down. She seemed oblivious to the fact that he was trying to go home.

"Some smart man is going to beat you to the punch if you're not careful," Louisa warned. "But then, I've given up matchmaking this year and have turned to more useful endeavors, such as baby-sitting." She patted the baby's back and then stepped away from the door. "Bring her back tomorrow night so you can go to the dance. Bring her little bed, too, so she can spend the night."

"I can't do that," Owen said, "but thanks for the offer. And thanks again for tonight."

He hurried outside and down the steps to where Darcy waited in the back seat of the truck.

He managed to get Mel settled in her seat and strapped in correctly without waking her up. "She should sleep all the way home."

Darcy leaned forward and put her head on his shoulder. "Uncle Owen?"

"Yeah?"

"I love you."

"I love you, too, Darce. Are you okay?"

"I miss Mom."

Owen drove in silence for a few minutes before he could answer. "Me, too."

"Are you going to get married?"

"I don't think anyone would have me." He thought of a woman with reddish-blond curls and a mouth that made him think of sex.

"Pam's mom got married again and they had to move to her stepfather's house in town and she hates it."

"We're not moving, not even if I have *three* wives." He hoped he could make her smile, but when he glanced into the rearview mirror, his niece still looked worried. "Darcy?"

"Hmm?"

"Nothing's going to change," he said, knowing that no matter what happened this week with Suzanne, it wasn't going to last.

"Promise?"

"Promise." He'd be lucky to see her again, much less be alone in the dark with her.

And, in the long run, it was probably better that way. He shouldn't get hot and bothered by a woman he couldn't have. He was more sensible than that.

At least, he used to be.

"I'M BEGINNING TO BE afraid the New York redhead is all wrong for him," Ella declared. The Hearts Club gathered for their weekly Saturday morning breakfast at the bowling alley coffee shop, where the cook made decent French toast and the waitress let them sit in the corner booth for as long as they wanted to.

Three pairs of eyebrows rose at this statement, but Grace was the only one to speak.

"I think she's lovely," she said, then hesitated. "But perhaps you know something we're not aware of, Ella?"

Ella set her coffee cup in its saucer and made her big announcement. "Owen lost his temper and almost hit Pete Peterson last night."

"Owen Chase would never hit someone more than twice his age," Louisa declared.

"I said he *almost* hit Pete. He realized who it was just in time, before he lost his temper." Ella had heard the story from Pete's sister, who lived three houses down from Ella and Louisa and walked her silly little dog every morning, in all kinds of weather, defiantly claiming her ski pole kept her from slipping on the ice.

"My goodness," Grace said. "He brought Suzanne home and they were in the truck for a few minutes— and you know what that means—"

Ella nodded, though she'd never been alone with a man in a car in all of her eighty-one years.

"And then I heard honking," Grace continued. "Before I knew it, Suzanne was at the door. I don't know what went on outside."

"Well, it just about scared Pete half to death," Ella said. "He'd only meant to honk as a joke—"

"The man has always had a terrible sense of humor," Missy interjected. "And that sister of his exaggerates. Last month she told me she invented Velcro, but someone stole her idea. Can you believe that?"

Grace shook her head. "What does all of this have to do with Suzanne Greenway and whether she'd be the right wife for Owen?"

Ella sighed. The sound of crashing bowling pins in the background made it difficult to think this morning. "Maybe we were too hasty. Perhaps we need to make a list of the available women—the ones we're aware of, not the strangers in town for the weekend—and go over other possibilities."

"Last night at dinner you said they looked wonderful together. I would think you'd be pleased that they were in Owen's truck last night." Missy reached into her purse for a pad and pen. "Do you think she's too forward a young woman for him?"

"We don't know anything about her," Ella agreed. "Maybe she's the sort of female who doesn't want to settle down at all."

"Do you think she'll break his heart?" Grace looked shocked. "I really don't think she's that sort at all, Ella. The girl keeps her room neat as a pin and she's very polite, too."

"Our Owen doesn't need to get himself tangled up with someone we don't know anything about." The red hair had led her off track, of course. The young lady was here for a story and that was that. Ella certainly didn't want Owen to get hurt. "If he gets hurt it will be our fault. I don't want that on my conscience."

"Too late," Grace said. "They fogged up the windows of his truck last night. And when was the last time you saw Owen Chase in town on a Friday night without his nieces?"

Louisa, who'd kept quiet and finished eating her breakfast, finally spoke. "He looked miserable last night," she declared. "He came to pick up the baby and he looked for all the world as if he didn't know what to do, as if his mind was somewhere else." She took a sip of her coffee. "Don't you think that's a good sign? Men in love tend to look somewhat ill, don't you agree?"

"Are you saying you took care of little Melanie?" Ella asked.

"Yes."

"Without telling me?"

"I don't tell you everything, Ella," her sister said in a very annoying tone. "Besides, you left for the supper early. Before I had my grand idea."

Ella didn't like the sound of this. "What grand idea would this be?"

"That the best way to find a match for Owen Chase was to take care of the baby so he'd be free to find a wife on his own," Louisa explained, looking a little too pleased with herself for Ella's peace of mind. "I have more ideas, too," she added.

"Oh, dear." Her older sister sighed. "That's what I'm afraid of, Lou."

"You have nothing to fear." Louisa looked at her friends. "I've given this a lot of thought, and I've decided that I not only will help Owen Chase, but I should find a husband for myself." She smiled. "Before it's too late."

Ella rolled her eyes. "I've got news for you, Sister. It's *already* too late."

"I'm not dead yet," Louisa declared. "When I'm not taking care of the baby, I'm going to look around for a man. I've decided that's why I've been so out of sorts lately. Life has passed me by."

"No, it hasn't," Ella protested, beginning to get annoyed with all of this nonsense. "We've led full and happy lives."

"Lives without sex," her sister said.

"Shh. For heaven's sake, keep your voice down."

"Ella, we're in a bowling alley."

Grace leaned forward. "Louisa, dear, sex is greatly overrated, believe me."

"No, it's not," Missy argued. "It's wonderful." The three women stared at her, which made Missy blush. "I was married for fifty-one years," she said, defending herself. "I should know."

"Well, I'll take your word for it, but I wouldn't mind finding out for myself," Louisa declared.

Ella wasn't the least bit amused by the turn the conversation had taken. "Well, good luck to you, Sister. Maybe you want to drive to the mall and buy some of that Victoria's Secret underwear."

"No," Lou said. "I sent for the catalog. You know I don't like driving on the interstate in the winter."

"But you're going to take care of a baby, find a man and have sex?" Ella reached for her water glass. "I think, as our father used to say, the world is going to hell in a handbasket."

"What exactly *is* a handbasket?" Missy asked.

Ella shrugged. "I don't know, but I imagine that if it exists we have several up in the attic."

"We have to clean that out," Lou murmured. "We should have a yard sale. Maybe we'll find something interesting to take on that television show where you find out how much your old things are worth."

"*Antiques Roadshow*," Grace said, and turned to Louisa. "You know, that might be a good place to meet men."

"Do I have to remind you how old you are, Louisa?" Ella had lost all patience. "The sex ship sailed without you decades ago."

Missy burst into laughter. "Ella, you are too funny."

"I'm serious. Could we please get back to the subject of Owen and potential Bliss women for him? I've had enough of this kind of talk."

"But Ella," Louisa said, winking at Missy. "Sex is what successful matchmaking is all about."

"Maybe we should take a vote," Grace suggested. "All those who wish to promote Suzanne raise your hand."

Three hands were raised, but Ella's fingers tapped her empty coffee cup.

"We could come up with other names, just in case," she said, wondering where she'd gone wrong.

"Let's give Suzanne a chance," Missy said.

"I agree." Grace wiped her mouth with her napkin and reached for her purse. "I'll do what I can from the house to promote the relationship, but Owen will have to make another move soon. She's a beautiful young lady who will get her share of attention."

"Yes," Ella agreed. That would be for the best. If Owen really had lost his temper, then he hadn't been himself last night, which meant the Greenway woman had him all stirred up. Owen didn't need to be stirred up; he needed a helpmate, a partner, a mother for the girls in his care. Ella did not want to think of the quiet and steady rancher in the same condition as a rutting bull.

"We'll do our best," her traitorous sister declared.

"I just want him to be happy," Ella told the others. "I want him to find the right woman."

Louisa reached over and patted her hand. "Don't feel badly, Ella. You can't be right all the time."

Except, Ella thought, she usually was. The problem was that people didn't always realize it at first.

STRICTLY BUSINESS, Suzanne decided. Her editor had loved the idea of a cowboy daddy on the cover of next year's November issue of *Romantic Living*, so that was what Suzanne would deliver.

There had to be other single-father types in Bliss. Owen Chase couldn't be the only one in this part of Montana. She wasn't going to follow the rancher around town as if she was some kind of love-struck female with nothing better to do than look for a man.

Unfortunately, her landlady was no help. She wasn't even around when Suzanne came downstairs for breakfast, so Suzanne helped herself to coffee and an applesauce muffin and ate alone in the dining room. She guessed that the other guests were wandering around town enjoying the sights and looking for love. Suzanne worked on her notes and organized the rest of her article until Mrs. Whitlow returned around midmorning.

"Are there any other single fathers in Bliss, men

like Owen Chase, I mean?" Suzanne hoped she sounded casual, as if she barely knew the man.

"Widowers?" Grace asked, acting as if she had never heard the word before. She set two bags of groceries on the counter and began to unload them. "I can't think of any off the top of my head."

"Mrs. Whitlow, I met someone named Gabe Thursday night at dinner. He's divorced?"

"His wife died," Grace said. "He's not the man for you, though."

"I'm not looking—"

"I meant for your article, honey. Gabe's pretty independent." Grace pointed to a gallon of milk. "Would you put that in the fridge for me? Thanks."

Suzanne did as she was told. Mrs. Whitlow's refrigerator was as spotless as the rest of her house. "How do you take care of this place all by yourself?"

"I taught home economics for forty years, so I know my way around a house. And I have help. Owen's girl, Darcy, cleans for me when she can." Grace looked at the clock on the wall above the window. "In fact, she should be here any minute." She smiled to herself and handed Suzanne a thick package of sliced turkey. "We'll invite the family for lunch. Won't that be nice? You and Owen can get to know each other a little better."

Suzanne took the food and set it on the counter. If

she and Owen knew each other any better, they'd have their clothes off.

The matchmakers would be shocked right down to their practical shoes.

6

"YOU'RE SUPPOSED TO COME in with me," Darcy said. "Mrs. Whitlow said she wanted to talk to you."

"About what?" Owen eyed the large white house and wondered where Suzanne was. Probably out prowling the streets of Bliss for happy couples to photograph. He parked the truck in the exact same place he'd parked it last night, and remembered exactly what it was like to kiss Suzanne.

He'd thought about that kiss many times during the night, had resolved not to do it again, and here he was. Sitting outside of the Whitlow house having an attack of nerves.

"I don't know what she wants," his niece answered. "But I'll bet it has something to do with the festival. You don't look too good, Uncle Owen. Are you sick?"

He shook his head. "I'm fine. Just thinking, that's all."

"Don't forget about tomorrow."

"Tomorrow?" Tomorrow was Sunday, but he couldn't remember making any plans.

"You're picking me up at Jen's house," Darcy reminded him. She gave him one of her looks that meant she thought he wasn't paying enough attention to the many important details of a teenage girl's life. She opened the truck door and began to round up her backpack and her duffel bag. "I'm going home with her tonight after practice to spend the night, and tomorrow we're working on our history project together."

"No problem."

"You won't forget about me, right?" She turned to him and her expression brightened.

"Nope. I promise." Owen was relieved to see her smile. Since her mother died, Darcy's smiles had been few and far between. And Owen didn't blame the girl; his sister's illness had drained the happiness out of the house. Thank God they'd had Melanie to put some joy back into their lives.

"Come on," the teenager said. "I need to get to work, and I'll bet Mrs. Whitlow is going to try to talk you into going to that dance tonight."

"It's the matchmaking season, all right," Owen said, turning around to get Mel out of her car seat. The baby grinned at him and showed her new tooth. "I hope I survive all the excitement."

"Oh, Uncle Owen." Darcy rolled her eyes. "You should go on a date or something. You really need to liven up a little."

"Like how?" He managed to get Mel settled against his chest and the truck door shut, then followed Darcy along the sidewalk and up the front steps. "Women aren't exactly lined up to go out with me, you know."

"I don't know about that. You're not that bad looking and you're not really *that* old. You could use some new clothes, though," she said, giving him a critical once-over. "I'm really sick of that shirt."

"I like this shirt." The brown-checked flannel was his favorite. "What's wrong with it?"

Darcy sighed. "I don't have time to explain it." With that depressing remark she turned away and knocked on the door.

"Hey, Mel," he said to his niece. "You have any complaints about my clothes?" The little girl babbled something and drooled on his collar. "I didn't think you did."

"Owen? Hi."

He hadn't heard the door open, certainly didn't expect Suzanne to greet them. Darcy said hi and swept past Suzanne into the house, but Owen hesitated. There was something about her that took his breath away, made words freeze in his throat while he stared into those blue eyes. She wore little makeup, and her hair was long and loose, falling past her shoulders. In a black turtleneck sweater, black slacks and black boots, she was the picture of sophisticated elegance, not a likely match for a silent rancher wearing an ugly shirt.

"Hello," he managed to answer, as Mel grabbed his ear and brought him to his senses.

"Come on in." Suzanne reached for the baby, her fingers brushing Owen's chest as the child turned to hold out her arms. "Hi, Melanie," she cooed, resting the child against her hip. She looked down at her and smiled. "You have red cheeks."

"It's a cold morning," Owen said, feeling stupid. It was Montana and it was November. What else would the weather be but cold? "Looks like snow," he added.

"Oh, good." Her attention shifted back to him. "I could get some great pictures of snow. Aren't you going to come in?"

"Well, I've got errands to run—"

Grace Whitlow had other ideas. "Not yet, Owen. I need your help with the dance tonight. You're going to be there, aren't you?"

"Well, I didn't—"

"If you don't see that our Suzanne here has a good time tonight, I'll just have to call one of the other bachelors on my list," Grace warned. "And I have a long list."

"I didn't intend to miss the dance," Owen lied. He'd changed his mind at least three hundred times since kissing Suzanne last night. "What kind of help do you need?"

"You're to introduce Suzanne to the town, keep Pete away from her and protect her from tourists and drunks," the woman announced. "And you're going to leave that little girl with me to spend the night, first of all. I'm not planning to go out tonight, because it's supposed to snow, and the last thing I want to do is fall down and break a hip."

"I'd be glad to see that you get there and back safely," Owen said. "And I can't leave Mel—"

"Oh, yes, you can, young man, because I have a spare room for you and Darcy, plus one of those portable cribs for the baby. You can spend the night, just like you were on vacation."

"I can't," he explained. "I've got animals to take care of."

"Well, you can't say I didn't try. But I'll take care of the baby while you're out, no arguing there." She shooed him into the dining room, where she'd arranged lunch.

Darcy poured coffee into three cups. "I'm spending the night with a friend, Mrs. Whitlow. We've got basketball practice later on."

"Well, doesn't that sound like fun," the elderly woman said. Then she turned to Suzanne. "You can put her in the high chair, if you don't mind. Then sit down, all of you, and help yourselves to a sandwich.

Darcy, you, too. Those beds can wait a few more minutes."

"Cool." Darcy set the coffee carafe on a hot pad in the center of the table and set a crystal sugar bowl in front of Grace's place. Owen wondered when she'd become so grown up. Suzanne managed to get Melanie settled in the high chair. He watched as she removed the child's pink coat and took off her hat. Melanie grinned and banged her fat little palms on the plastic tray, which made Suzanne laugh and Owen want to take both of them in his arms.

"Suzanne, tell us a little bit about yourself." Mrs. Whitlow handed her a plate of sandwiches. "Have you always lived in New York?"

"I grew up in Connecticut, with my aunt and uncle," she added too casually. "My parents died when I was ten. I have two older sisters—both married with children—and I live in New York City now."

Darcy leaned forward, her gaze on Suzanne's face. "So you're like me," she said. She might as well have added "an orphan," but Suzanne appeared to know what the teenager meant.

"Yes," she said. "It's not easy, is it?"

"No." Darcy took a deep breath. "Connecticut is near New York, right?" Darcy looked impressed. "That's a long way away from Montana."

"It certainly is," Suzanne agreed. "But what about you? What do you do around here for fun?"

"Mostly just school and sports. And I have a horse."

She handed Suzanne the basket of potato chips. "Uncle Owen and I used to ride a lot when Grandma lived with us."

"Darcy's father's mother," Owen explained.

"Suzanne, tell Owen where you're going this afternoon. I'm sure he can help you with whatever you need."

"Are you matchmaking, Mrs. Whitlow?" Suzanne asked. She didn't seem to mind Grace's unabashed attempt to throw them together, Owen noted.

"Of course. It's festival season. The Hearts Club met for breakfast this morning and discussed our plans."

"The Hearts Club?"

"Just four of us who play cards," Grace explained. "You've met Louisa and Ella. You'll most likely meet Missy Perkins tonight."

"No one's safe," Owen told Suzanne. He hoped he sounded casual and lighthearted. Like Gabe. Or Calder. "It'll be over in less than two weeks, then everything will be back to normal."

He told himself he had to be optimistic. He told himself he didn't need to get involved with a woman—any kind of woman—right now. He even told himself that he didn't want a woman who wasn't going to stick around.

And Owen knew he was telling himself a whole bucketful of lies.

"YOU DON'T HAVE TO DO this," Suzanne said. Main Street was crowded with tourists, much busier on a Saturday than a weekday. Many were couples, while others strolled in groups of three and four. The men easily outnumbered the women. "I don't think I could get lost on Main Street."

"You're making Grace Whitlow happy," Owen said. "She's on the phone with the Bliss sisters right now, telling them she engineered this."

"The women take this all very seriously," Suzanne said. "Do you think the town really does have a kind of wedding good-luck charm about it?"

He groaned. "Not you, too."

"What do you mean?"

"The local paper publishes a list of successful marriages at the end of every year and compares our low divorce rate to the rest of the country. They think there's something in the water. And then there was a psychic from California here a few years ago who claimed the entire town had an aura."

Suzanne pulled her notebook from her jacket pocket. "What kind of aura?"

"The kind brought on by too many margaritas."

"Oh." She wrote down "aura?" anyway and readied her camera. "Why don't you and Mel stand over there, by the Marryin' Sam's sign? It would make a great picture."

He frowned at her. "No, it wouldn't."

"You could be on the cover of *Romantic Living* next year," she said, knowing that Owen wouldn't care one way or the other about that. But she wanted the picture for herself, a souvenir to remember Bliss by.

"I don't want to be on the cover of anything." He continued to frown down at her. "I'd have to get a new shirt."

She stopped in front of the window of Bliss Outfitters and pointed to the display of men's clothing. "So get a new shirt."

"What's the matter with the one I'm wearing?"

"I have no idea, especially because it's covered up by your jacket." Owen clearly didn't know how appealing he was, all male and buckskin and leather, pushing a stroller that held a chubby baby wearing pink. No woman in her right mind would complain about Owen's shirt, whatever it looked like. "Do you *want* a new shirt?"

"No."

"Then stand over there and let me take the picture. It won't go in the magazine and I'll send you a copy for Mel's baby book. You're wearing a jacket. The shirt won't even show." Owen didn't look enthused, but he positioned the stroller and the baby where she directed.

"Then we're heading back," he said. "I've got chores to do."

"Would you like me to take the picture for you?"

Suzanne lowered the camera and turned to see a young couple step around her on the sidewalk. The young woman dropped her husband's hand.

"That way you can all be in it," she said.

"Oh, I don't need..." Suzanne began, then stopped. "Thanks. That would be great." She explained what button to push, adjusted the focus, then walked over to Owen to pose.

"One, two, three, *smile*," the woman said, while her husband looked on. Suzanne smiled and wondered what Owen's expression would be. Tortured, probably.

"Thanks," Suzanne said, when the woman returned the camera. "Are you here for the festival?"

"We met here last year, so we thought we'd come back for our honeymoon."

"Really." They looked so young. And so happy. And they made Suzanne remember how much she detested weddings and happy couples. She'd become cranky and cynical and she wasn't even thirty years old yet.

"Congratulations," she remembered to say as the couple walked off, hand in hand once again.

"What was that all about?" Owen asked when she returned to the stroller.

"They're on their honeymoon," she explained. "Bliss worked its spell once again. It's unbelievable."

"After a while you get used to it," Owen said. "We get a lot of honeymooners around here."

"What about you?" she asked, crossing the street beside him. "Don't *you* want to get married someday?"

"It's not that simple," he said.

"Why not?"

He took his time answering while they headed back to Mrs. Whitlow's house. "I've got two kids to raise. Any decisions I make affects them."

"I can understand that," Suzanne said, "but don't you get lonely?"

He stopped pushing the stroller and turned to look down at her. "Well, hell. Sure I do. But I'm waiting for the right woman to come along."

The "right woman" would be very lucky to have this man in her life, Suzanne knew. Because after last night she also knew that Owen's calm exterior hid a man of great passion. Then again, she was better off forgetting about last night. She walked a little faster and attempted to remember she was a writer, not a prospective candidate for marriage, thank goodness.

But still, Owen Chase would make someone a good husband someday. She only hoped the woman would deserve him.

HE WONDERED WHAT he'd done to deserve this. The Grange dance lasted from seven until ten, so the older folks in town could enjoy an early evening. The band, Country Joe and His Pardners, looked as if they might die of old age between the first and second sets. The crowd was a sea of gray hair and Stetsons, the air scented with roses and Old Spice.

Owen figured if he was smart, he never would have agreed to do this. A more intelligent man, one with a greater sense of self-preservation, would have stayed home and watched television or gotten caught up on the account books. He'd have read that latest article on irrigation techniques and rocked Mel to sleep and then fried himself a steak. At least he wasn't going to spend the night in town; he and Mel would be going home to their own beds, and not a moment too soon, either. He still didn't feel right leaving Mel with Grace Whitlow, but the baby hadn't seemed to mind. He'd called once already, getting Grace's assurance that she'd track him down at the Grange or the "Blues" bar if there was an emergency. She could always call the sheriff; everyone knew Owen's truck.

He just wasn't used to going out, that was all. If he'd stayed home he would not be dancing around the room with Ella Bliss. He was afraid if he stepped on her foot she would shatter into a hundred pieces and end up limping to her grave.

"Now, Owen," she said. "Callie is a perfectly lovely young woman. A little lively, but you could do a lot worse."

"Yes, ma'am," he said, knowing darn well that Callie was in one of the bars outside of town torturing young cowboys. He looked over to see Suzanne dance past in Pete Peterson's arms. Pete looked pretty happy with himself and probably figured he'd like to marry a redhead this time around. Owen didn't like the way Suzanne smiled at the old guy, as if she thought he was harmless.

Harmless, my ass.

"And then there's my neighbor's granddaughter, but she hasn't arrived in town yet," Ella said. Owen concentrated on his two-step. "Wouldn't you like to meet her?"

"I don't have a lot of time for dating, Ella. In fact, I hadn't planned on being here tonight, but—"

"Grace coerced you," she finished for him. "I know all about it, and I want you to understand that you don't have to squire the Greenway woman around any longer."

"I don't?" He made a careful turn, intending to keep Suzanne within sight.

"The whole town is talking about your punching Peterson last night, you know."

Owen chuckled. "I didn't punch anyone."

"His sister said...well, never mind."

"I told him to stop honking his horn. Turned out he'd been drinking." The tipsy old man, unaware he'd interrupted Owen's idea of heaven, had been trying to get Suzanne's attention. "I ended up driving him home."

"Oh."

"Check him out," Owen said. "No bruises anywhere on him."

Ella craned her neck and then looked up at him. "I do apologize for repeating rumors, Owen."

"No problem." The music came to an end, his dance partner was immediately surrounded by several senior citizens, and Owen was free to pursue—against his better judgment—the woman he'd brought to this event.

"Pete spiked the punch," Suzanne whispered, sipping something from a paper cup. "I think he put rum in it when Louisa turned her back."

"He didn't propose to you again, did he?"

"Only twice." She smiled and drank some more. "He promised me my own horse. And my own truck."

"And your own old man in your bed," Owen added. "What a deal."

"Hey," she protested, when he lifted the cup from her hand and tossed it in the garbage. "What are you doing?"

"Taking you to experience another kind of matchmaking," he said. He took her hand and led her through the crowd and into the foyer. He found both of their coats, led her to the parking lot, settled her inside the truck and headed out of town.

"Well?"

"What?" He glanced over to see her pulling on her gloves.

"Where are we going?"

"To the Wedding Bell Blues Bar and Grill," he explained. "Where the real action is."

"Oh, good."

He sure as hell didn't mind having her all to himself. There was something about being alone with her that made him want to pull her into his arms and kiss her until neither one of them could breathe. And that was only the first part of his alone-in-the-night fantasy.

Maybe Gabe was right. He should get out more.

"I don't know how to line dance," she said, when they'd pulled up near the bar. It was a large building and the sound coming from inside was pure country. Despite the cold, a lot of people hung around outside, smoking cigarettes and drinking beer. "I think you should know that before we go inside."

"What's that got to do with anything?"

"It looks like the kind of place where everyone knows all the fancy steps."

"You can two-step, right?" He turned off the engine and tried not to look at her. She was a reporter, not his date. He was only with her because of the misguided matchmaking of several elderly ladies. Because he'd made that stupid crack about wanting a woman with red hair.

Because he couldn't stay away from her.

"Well, yes. Sort of." She sounded a little uncertain, so he made the mistake of turning toward her. Which meant, since she was so close, that her hair was inches from his fingertips. Which meant he couldn't resist touching her shoulder. He fingered one curl, gave it a gentle tug, watched her eyes widen and her lips soften, and then he was kissing her again as if he'd been waiting all day to feel that mouth of hers under his. It would be so easy to unbutton her coat and slide his hands along that black sweater, but Owen remembered that he was in his truck. In front of a bar. With an audience. It just about killed him to end the kiss. In fact, he couldn't quite manage it, so his fingers held her head still while he drew his lips along her jaw, to that soft little hollow behind her ear and back, to find her mouth again.

The crash of a beer bottle reminded him where he was, which was not in his bed where he could do all the things he wanted to do with this woman. For now he would have to settle for dancing, so he lifted his head and smoothed her hair with his fingers. And he tried to sound casual.

"Come on, then. Let's see if we can find some happy dancing couples for your story." He opened his door and hopped out. A few of the men nodded to him; a few more looked surprised to see him at the "Blues" on a Saturday night.

"Chase," one said, tossing his cigarette onto the gravel. "Nice evenin'."

"Sure is." Owen took a proprietary hold on Suzanne's arm, making it clear that the woman was with him and not up for grabs.

"Makin' a night of it, are ya?" another asked.

"Sure am," was all Owen said, but his meaning was clear: I'm here with my woman and the rest of you can damn well back off.

All of a sudden Owen Chase was having one hell of a good time.

7

"I SEE A LOT OF POTENTIAL wives here," Suzanne said, surveying the enormous, crowded room.

There was a bar on each side, a band playing at one end of a packed dance floor, and people everywhere. She'd never seen so many cowboys together in one place in all of her life, except for the time she'd watched a few minutes of a rodeo on television. If ever there was a place to meet a member of the opposite sex, this was it.

Owen ignored the comment and guided her through the noisy crowd. When he reached the bar he bent down. "What do you want to drink?"

If she tilted her head, her lips would graze his cheek. So she tilted her head and figured she'd live dangerously, at least for a while. She should never have kissed him again, but there was something about the man she couldn't resist, though she knew she should try harder. The truth was she felt a little lonely these days. And a little too pathetic for her own good, come to think of it, an insight that made her thirsty.

"Rum and Coke," she told him, her lips touching his skin ever so lightly, and hoped he could hear the words over the sound of the music.

"Stay close," he said. He put one arm around her shoulder and held her in front of him, protecting her from being jostled or elbowed. He was a large man, so he easily managed to make an opening in the crowd and get them close enough to the bar to catch the bartender's eye.

It was like standing in front of a tree trunk. His large hands rested casually on her shoulders, another protective gesture that was both comforting and sensual at the same time. Once they had their drinks, Owen managed to find two empty bar stools. So Suzanne sipped her drink, watched the dancing and felt as if she'd fallen into another world. There were an awful lot of people having a very good time at this bar, and many of them appeared to know each other.

"Getting some more ideas for your story?" someone asked, and Suzanne turned to see Callie.

"I wish I had my camera," Suzanne answered. "I have to get a picture of you before I leave town. Can I interview you for the magazine?"

"Anytime. My grandmother can tell you how and where to find me." Callie, gorgeous in tight faded jeans and a white, Western-style shirt, looked flushed and happy, as if she'd been dancing all night, and when the bartender handed her a bottle of beer, she took a long swallow before greeting Owen.

"Hey, Owen," she said. "It's pretty wild seeing you here. Two nights in a row you're out socializing? Wow."

"I've decided to get out more," he replied.

"Me, too," she said, and laughed before turning to Suzanne. "I've had three proposals so far tonight," she said. "One decent and two indecent. I'm not sure which one I'll accept."

"Stay out of trouble," Owen said, but he smiled. "And try not to break any hearts."

"Too late." Callie grinned, clearly having had more than one drink. "I may set a new record this weekend. See ya later," she said, moving toward the dance floor. "And have fun."

"Come on," Owen said, as the band started a new song. "Let's dance."

"Nothing fancy, right?" Suzanne set her drink on the bar for safekeeping and hopped down from the stool.

"Nothing fancy," he promised, and took her hand. "It's a slow one. An old Willie Nelson song called 'Crazy.'"

"Oh?" She passed a lot of very good-looking young men. If her single friends in New York could see this, they'd move West. And she realized that was the point of all those mail-order brides years ago. Horace Bliss had been onto something, all right.

"You do know who Willie Nelson is, don't you?" Owen led her onto the dance floor and tugged her into his arms, which, she decided, was a very nice place to be.

"I don't have a clue," she admitted, resisting the temptation to rest her head against his chest. She was dancing with a real cowboy, one who wore jeans and boots and knew whatever there was to know about cattle and land and dancing in bars on Saturday nights.

"Seriously?" His breath tickled her ear.

She looked up at him. "Sorry. You're dancing with a city girl, remember?"

"Yeah," he said, and looked as if he was going to kiss her.

"You can't," she said, realizing that where this man was concerned she had no willpower to resist. There really must be something in the air here in Montana, she decided. Or in the coffee.

"Can't what?"

"Kiss me anymore."

His gaze dropped to her lips. "But I like kissing you."

"That's the problem. You're supposed to find a wife, not have...well, not get sidetracked with me."

"Hmm," was all he said, but he tucked her closer

against him, against that long length of hard male, and Suzanne wanted nothing more than to curl her hands around his neck. Luckily, she remembered she shouldn't do that.

Unfortunately, Owen had other ideas. He dropped both hands to her waist, leaving her no choice but to loop her arms around his neck. Loosely, of course. She didn't want to encourage him, but this actually was a more comfortable way of dancing slow. The dance floor had become so crowded that they could barely move, which made everything worse. It made her even more aware of how nicely their bodies fit together.

And made her wish she hadn't drunk quite so much rum punch at the Grange.

When the song finally ended, Owen released her, but the band moved quickly into another slow song, so Suzanne went into his arms as naturally as if she did this every Saturday night.

"How do you like the place so far?" he asked.

"It's very nice," she managed to say, aware that she was living dangerously. Owen Chase might be a loving uncle, patient with elderly ladies and a good friend to everyone in the state of Montana, but he was still a man. And, if she wasn't mistaken, a man who wanted her—in the physical sense, of course.

"It'll get busier as the night goes on," he said. "If

you want to interview anyone, it might be a good idea to do it before folks get too drunk."

"Good idea." Talking to some Montana couples would give her a reason to avoid any more of this slow dancing with Owen. There was a lot to be said for sexual attraction, but Suzanne had no intention of ending up in bed with a cowboy, or anyone else, for that matter. Casual sex wasn't her style, even if she hadn't the resolve to stay away from relationships for a long, long time.

His embrace tightened a little more, and this time Suzanne rested her head against his shoulder. She grew all too aware of his hands on her waist, his fingers splayed on her hips. If he moved his hands lower, she would be in real trouble.

The dance ended just in time, before her knees grew too shaky to hold her up.

"Are you *sure* you don't want to get married?" Owen murmured as he released her and stepped back.

"What?" She prayed he wasn't serious, that he wasn't going to ruin the evening and propose to her himself.

"You're attracting a lot of attention," he explained, and she realized from the twinkle in his eyes that he was teasing her. "If I left you alone for a few minutes, you'd meet your share of bachelors. You might even be offered more than your own horse and truck in exchange for a wedding."

"I can take care of myself," she replied, but she kept her hand in his as they left the dance floor and headed across the room to claim their drinks. "But what about you? Don't you want to make the Bliss ladies happy and find a wife? I'm cramping your style."

"I don't want a wife," Owen said. He lowered his head so she would be sure to hear him, and his lips grazed her ear. "I want *you.*"

"You really can't—"

The band burst into a loud, fast song, preventing Suzanne from saying anything else, not that she knew what to say. Her body was screaming one thing, while her brain had completely shut down.

Owen switched directions, passed the bar and headed for a set of double doors. The doors opened into a long hallway, with rest room signs and a pay phone on the wall.

"Okay," he said, looking down at her. "Now we can talk. I can't *what?*"

"Can't have me."

"Why not?"

"Well, I can't have you, either," she answered, hoping that she was making some kind of sense, yet knowing she wasn't. "The matchmakers should get busy and find you someone else."

"I've been kissing you. And you've been kissing me back."

"Yes. And I shouldn't have. I'm really sorry about that."

He didn't look convinced. He almost looked as if he wanted to laugh. "You're sorry," he repeated.

"Yes. Very." She backed up against the pine-paneled wall to let two women pass by on their way from the ladies' room. Owen rested his palms on either side of her head and was suddenly very close as he studied her face.

"You're a very beautiful woman, but I guess you know that," he said.

"Thank you."

"You're welcome." His mouth descended; his lips brushed her temple.

"Maybe we shouldn't dance anymore." Suzanne didn't know what to do with her hands. Hooking her fingers into his belt and pulling his bottom half against her would not be a good idea, so she shoved her hands in the pockets of her slacks, just for safety's sake.

"That might help," he agreed, feathering light kisses down to her ear, her jaw, toward her mouth. "And we should stay out of my truck, too."

"Absolutely." She turned her head so her mouth met his, and for several searing seconds forgot everything she might have said a moment before.

When he lifted his mouth, Suzanne ignored every impulse to wrap her arms around him and pull him to her.

"I could walk home," she whispered, and watched his lips slant into a smile.

"Good idea." He kissed the corner of her mouth ever so lightly. "We shouldn't be alone together."

"No. Absolutely not." She closed her eyes and gave thanks she was in a public place. Despite the fact that his hands remained on the wall, Owen had a way of kissing that made her wonder if having sex against a wall in a Montana bar wasn't such a bad idea, after all, but she assumed he'd have more restraint.

"Okay." And of course he kissed her again, and this time she took her hands from her pockets and slid them along his wide chest. She felt his heartbeat under her right palm, the heat emanating from his body, and she urged him closer, so that hard male body was against hers.

"Hey, guys, get a room," a female voice called, and the sound of women's laughter grew louder as they walked past on their way to the bathroom.

"Not a bad idea," Owen said, lifting his head. He straightened, stepped back and took her hand. "I'm glad we got that settled."

"No rooms. No kissing. No truck. No beds." She didn't know if she was reminding him or herself.

"You sure know how to take the fun out of a Saturday night. Come on." He tugged her hand and led her back through the doors and into the main room, where they joined the crowd dancing to a lively song about Texas. The band sounded louder, the place more crowded, and most of the people there looked like they didn't want to be anywhere else.

Suzanne did. She wanted to get out of the bar, the town and the state as soon as possible. Falling in love—or falling in lust—with Owen Chase was completely out of the question.

ELLA DIDN'T KNOW WHAT Louisa saw in that old man. Peterson drank too much, laughed too loud and proposed marriage to anything in a skirt. And there was her sister, hopping around the dance floor with him as if it was the 1940s all over again. When the music finally stopped, her sister came over and sat down with her at their table.

"Louisa," Ella hissed, making the candle in the centerpiece quiver. "You're going to give yourself a heart attack."

Her plump twin fanned herself with a napkin while the band took one of its long breaks between sets. "I'm having fun, Ella.. You should try it sometime."

"I have fun." Really, Louisa was in danger of hurting her feelings if she kept this up. "Besides, we're supposed to be matchmaking, not monopolizing the single men."

"There aren't too many single men here, Ella, so who are we supposed to be coaching? Look around you. This party ends in twenty minutes—less, if the band doesn't come back in time—and there's no one under sixty-five left in the building. That leaves about thirty women with ten men to dance with until it's time to go home and watch the weather report on the late news. Us old-timers—single or not single— are merely having a good time."

"I suppose any couples who made a connection tonight have already left." Ella sighed, thinking of Owen and Suzanne. "Suzanne left with Owen Chase tonight, so you must be pleased."

"That pairing is off to a good start," Louisa agreed. "I suppose they went on to one of the saloons outside of town."

"I suppose. Or maybe he took her home."

"Home?" Louisa beamed with satisfaction.

"I meant, delivered her to Grace's, safe and sound. Owen Chase can't be taking women back to the ranch where the children are, you know." And that led to a problem Ella hadn't considered when it came to Owen: privacy. No matter who he dated, it would be difficult for them to spend time alone together.

"Grace said the older girl is spending the night

with a friend. Grace even offered a room to Owen and the baby, but he refused," Lou related.

"So the ranch is empty," Ella stated, imagining all sorts of improper goings-on. She wasn't quite sure she approved of all of this premarital sex that went on these days, but then again, she assumed when it came to sex she hadn't missed much. "When is our reporter leaving town?"

"I have no idea, Ella. I assumed she was going to stay the entire two weeks, but perhaps she won't. I don't know anything about writers, do you?"

"Ask Grace tomorrow. We either have to assume Suzanne's the right woman for him and throw them together, or decide she's an unnecessary distraction and move in another direction. Those girls need a mother."

"You're the only one of us with doubts, Sister. The others are ready to move forward." Louisa dabbed her lace-edged hankie into her water glass, then wiped her face. "And I wish we could hurry the process along a bit, so I could concentrate on finding a man for myself."

"Good Lord," Ella groaned. "Not that again."

Louisa fanned the air above her plump breasts. "I may be old, but I'm not dead yet."

Ella looked past her sister to see their ancient neighbor approaching them. She looked at her sister and shook her head. "You may want to pretend, dear, or have to listen to old Cameron tell you about his stamp collection again."

"At least it shows he's passionate about something," Louisa retorted, which was the last straw for Ella. She nodded to Cameron when he reached the table. "Hello, Cam. Hit any school buses lately?"

He stared at her and cupped his ear. "Eh?"

"*Wonderful music*," she shouted.

"Yes, yes, good," the old man said. "And how are you, Ella?"

"Fine, Cam. *Just fine.*" She picked up her empty punch cup and stood.

"Where are you going?" Louisa asked.

"To ask Peterson if there's any more of that rum left. I suddenly feel the need for alcohol."

"Go for it," her sister said. "And if he asks you to dance, say yes. He can really get your blood pumping."

"My blood is fine where it is," Ella replied. "I'll meet you at the front door at ten o'clock. Don't be late. Tomorrow's going to be another big day."

Her sister paid no attention to her, but Cameron looked a little disappointed at her departure. Well, he'd get over it, Ella knew. He'd had his chance sixty years ago.

MEANWHILE, back at the "Blues", Owen realized he might have made a very big mistake. He'd talked

Suzanne out of leaving early by asking the bartender if there was anything special going on in the bar tonight. Sure enough, as was typical of festival time, another wedding was about to begin.

"A wedding? Here?" Suzanne looked as if she'd won the lottery.

"That's right," said the bartender. "It's the season, you know. We've got another wedding and reception scheduled at eleven, for a couple from Grand Forks who met here a year ago today and wanted to get married in the same place, at the same time. Pretty cool, huh?"

"Very. Do you think they'd let me have an interview?"

"You can ask," the kid said, pointing to a crowd gathered across the room. "They're over there getting ready."

"My notebook's in your truck," she told Owen. "Would you mind giving me your keys so I—"

"Stay right here," Owen said, knowing she shouldn't be walking through the parking lot by herself. "I'll get it."

"And my camera, too? Don't bother bringing the whole purse. It'll just get in my way," she said, smiling at him. "And thanks."

"Sure." There was no way in hell he was going to walk back into the bar carrying a purse. He wasn't real crazy about toting Mel's diaper bag around, but at least he could fit an extra bottle of milk and a disposable diaper or two in the large front pockets of his winter coat when he had to. Owen paused before leaving Suzanne alone at the bar. "Just stay right here, okay?"

"If I'm not here, look for me at the wedding," she said, completely unaware of what an appealing picture she made perched on that bar stool. "I don't want to miss a thing."

He found her in the crowd ten minutes later. She was surrounded by cowboys of varying heights and ages, and when he made his way to her side she smiled up at him in a way that made him wish he could haul her out of there and have her all to himself.

"I usually hate weddings," she said, "but this is fun."

"Rum helps," he said, noting she held a fresh drink. "Here are your things."

"Thanks." She took the camera and slung the strap over her shoulder, then tucked the notebook under her arm.

"Here." He pulled her bright pink pen from his pocket and handed it to her.

"You're a good man to have around," she said, giving him a quick smile before turning away to watch the wedding.

Then keep me around, he wanted to say, but he

never got the chance. The wedding music started and Suzanne's attention was focused on the bride, a buxom brunette who beamed with joy. The groom grinned from ear to ear underneath his brand-new Stetson and kissed his bride when she joined him in front of the minister. Owen didn't know either one of them, though he recognized a few faces in the crowd of onlookers. Gabe wasn't around, which was no surprise, since he didn't frequent the "Blues." And Calder, afraid of no man but terrified of the Bliss sisters, had hightailed it out of town right before the festival began.

So here stood Owen, at the top of the matchmakers' hit list, playing chaperon to a reporter who kissed like an angel and yet hated weddings—up until this one. A man was supposed to feel relieved when a woman didn't show any interest in marriage, and here he was, all dejected and frustrated because he couldn't get her to take him seriously.

He wanted Suzanne in his bed. Plain and simple. And by the looks on the faces of the cowboys Suzanne was now talking to, other men wouldn't mind taking her home, either. Pretty soon one of them would volunteer to be the bachelor she'd follow around for a few days, and that would be the end of Owen Chase. As far as the reporter was concerned, he'd be old news.

As soon as the short ceremony ended and the onlookers broke into applause, Owen waded back into the crowd and claimed a spot beside Suzanne. He knew she wanted a bachelor for her story, so maybe he'd have to pretend he wanted a wife.

"Nice wedding," he said.

"I'm going to try to interview the bride later on," Suzanne told him. "The groom was almost too nervous to talk."

"Most guys are."

She fussed with her camera and put it back in its case. "Yes," she said, sounding uncharacteristically bitter. "Well, at least he had the nerve to show up."

"Why wouldn't he?" Owen realized he didn't know very much about this woman, but she'd said she hated weddings, which seemed a little strange, considering the way women usually behaved at these things.

Suzanne shrugged. "Six months ago mine didn't. Show up, I mean."

"You were at the *church?*" Owen couldn't quite fathom any sane man walking out on the chance to be with this woman.

"I sure was." She took a sip of her drink. "Thank goodness I hadn't put the dress on yet."

"What did you do?" He stood as close as he dared, hoping the music wouldn't start up right away, so he could hear.

Suzanne shrugged. "I threw up on the best man."

He wanted to ask where the creep was that had let her down, wanted to know why he hadn't married her, and wanted to thank him for leaving her free to come to Bliss and be with him.

Owen kept his mouth shut and took Suzanne's free hand. "Come on," he said as the music started up. "They're playing a waltz."

"How romantic," she murmured, sounding as if she meant it.

"That's right." He tucked her against his body after they stepped onto the dance floor. "Romance is what Bliss is all about."

She laughed. "That is the silliest thing I've ever heard you say."

"I'm trying to come up with good quotes for your article." She fit against him perfectly. All he had to do was remember he had to pick up his baby in an hour and couldn't ask Suzanne to come home with him for a night of passionate sex.

8

SHE CAUGHT THE BRIDAL bouquet.

"I didn't mean to," she said, holding on to the thing as if it was a dead rat. "It just came out of nowhere."

"Nice catch," Owen said. "Maybe you'll find a husband here in Bliss, after all."

"No, thanks," Suzanne replied, trying to give the little bouquet of white daisies and chrysanthemums to the young woman on the bar stool next to her. The woman shook her head and held up her hands as if to ward off evil. "I don't need the bad luck, either."

"Do you still love him?" Owen asked.

"Who?" She set the floral thing behind her on the bar and picked up her drink.

"The guy you wanted to marry."

"No." After she'd gotten over the shock and the anger and the tears, she'd realized she was better off without the jerk in the first place, just as her aunt and uncle had pronounced. Her pride stung, and her ego, too. She'd thought Greg was perfect in every way—something he agreed with totally—until the romantic haze wore off. "I discovered afterward that I didn't miss him very much." She made a face at Owen, a man she was afraid she'd miss very much once she returned to civilization. "Could we change the subject?"

"We have to leave, anyway," the rancher said. "It's almost midnight and I told Grace—"

"We'd be home before twelve," Suzanne finished for him. She hopped off the stool and gathered her belongings, pushed her unfinished drink aside and picked up the bouquet.

"I thought you didn't want it," he said.

"You can give it to your niece. She'll probably think it's cool."

"Probably. Not much makes her happy these days." He retrieved their coats from one of the hooks by the door and made sure Suzanne was bundled up before they went outside. Snow greeted them, coming down in fat flakes that barely covered the street.

"She must miss her mother terribly," Suzanne said, remembering what it was like to lose her parents. "That never goes away."

"No."

"What about her father?" she asked, once they had reached the truck.

"I don't know who he was," Owen answered. He unlocked the passenger door and held it open for her. "My sister never said and I never asked. She married a nice guy from Bozeman a few years back, but he was killed in a freak train accident right before Mel was born."

"I'm so sorry," Suzanne said, wondering how she could think a canceled wedding was any kind of tragedy after hearing about Owen's family. "For all of you."

He lifted her chin and smiled at her. "We're doing okay, so don't look so sad. Even Darcy's starting to smile more now."

Suzanne wanted to kiss him, she really did. But she'd decided that touching him in any way was just asking for trouble. So she moved her head and broke contact with him as if she hadn't known he wanted to kiss her, right there in the fresh, cold air while snowflakes fell and dusted his dark hair.

"Gosh, it's cold," she said, sounding like an idiot as she turned away and fumbled with her seat belt. Owen shut her door and went around the truck while Suzanne leaned over and unlocked the door for him. The interior of the truck really was frigid. If she lived here she'd buy insulated boots and a down-filled jacket. *If she lived here?* What on earth was the matter with her? Suzanne shivered.

"It'll take a few minutes to warm up," Owen said, as he started the engine. And that was the extent of the conversation on the way back to town. She'd gone too far, dancing and kissing and snuggling in the truck...talking and laughing and catching that bridal bouquet. She needed to go back to her room, check her e-mail, play a few games of solitaire on the laptop and plan what more she needed to do in Bliss before she got the hell out of town.

She didn't know that Owen's baby would have other ideas.

Grace met them at the door and held her finger to her lips. "The little dear is finally asleep," she whispered. "I don't want her to hear your voice."

"Did she give you any trouble?" Owen wiped his boots on the welcome mat inside the door.

"She was a little fussy. I think she's getting another tooth," Grace said. "But she's sleeping like a little darling now. I rocked her and sang to her and we made out just fine." She looked at the snow on Suzanne's hair. "Oh, my. Is it snowing again?"

"Just started," Owen said. "I'd better be getting back home before it gets any worse."

Grace shook her head. "Now, Owen, you know it's not right to take that child out of her bed. If she wakes up she'll be miserable again, I'm sure. Why don't you just stay? The spare room's all made up for you."

Owen smiled. "I can't, Grace. I've got animals to look after, but I appreciate the offer. Mel will settle down once she's in the truck and we're heading home. She never minds riding."

"But the snow," Grace said.

"And her tooth," Suzanne added. "Let her stay, Owen," she heard herself say.

"Come see for yourself how comfy she is," Grace said, motioning them to follow her up the stairs. "I keep a little portable crib on hand for my guests, and your little girl seemed to like it once she settled down." At the end of the long hall and around a corner was another door, and Mrs. Whitlow carefully opened it and tiptoed inside, with Suzanne and Owen close behind.

The baby lay sprawled on her stomach, the lace-edged collar of her pajamas peeking above the pastel quilt. She was clearly sound asleep and very peaceful. The room was large, with a queen-size bed piled high with quilts, two oak dressers and a rocking chair in the corner. A bathroom could be seen through a door across the room.

Owen bent down and studied the child, then tucked the quilt higher around her neck and lightly patted her back. He straightened and shrugged as if he didn't know what to do. Grace shooed them out of the room and into the hall.

"See?" she whispered. "You can't possibly be thinking of taking that child out in a blizzard."

"It's not exactly a blizzard," Owen said, keeping his voice low. "But I get your point." He sighed. "What if she wakes up in the middle of the night?

There'll be no one to hear. Or she'll wake up the rest of your guests."

"I'll stay with her," Suzanne said, at the same time wondering what she was doing, getting involved in something that was none of her business. "I'll move some of my things in here. That way she won't be alone and I can hear her if she wakes up. Does she get a bottle?"

Owen and Grace stared at her.

"I have two nieces and a nephew," Suzanne said. "All under age six."

"I can't let you do that," Owen said, all of a sudden looking very tired.

"Go home," she said, still whispering as they walked toward the stairs. "Come back in the morning when your cows are fed, and pick her up." She turned to Grace. "Do we have enough diapers?"

"I brought extra," Owen replied. "And there's plenty of formula in the diaper bag. In cans."

"Okay."

"She'll probably wake up around five, but if she's had a tough night, she'll sleep later." He pulled on his gloves and turned to Grace. "You've got my phone number, right?"

"I sure do," Grace said, patting him on the back. "Go home, son, and get some rest. You look like you could use it."

That made him smile, so when he turned toward

Suzanne she was struck by what a fine looking man he was. Not your typical model kind of handsome, all bones and taut skin, but a solid kind of handsome that made a woman want to hold him to her and never let him go.

Suzanne blinked. "Go," she said. "Don't worry about a thing."

"Thanks," he said, and with one long step was close enough to bend down and kiss her. It was the briefest of kisses, just a slight brushing of lips, but Suzanne felt the jolt all the way down to her frozen toes.

And then he was gone, leaving Grace Whitlow looking very pleased with herself.

"I can't wait to tell Louisa," she muttered, glancing at a grandfather's clock near the foot of the stairs. "Too bad it's so late."

"No more matchmaking, Mrs. Whitlow," Suzanne warned. "I'm only doing the man a favor, which doesn't qualify me as someone who'd marry him."

"But he kissed you."

"It was just a little thank-you-for-baby-sitting kiss. Do you think I should take a bottle upstairs now, just in case she wakes up?"

"Owen Chase doesn't go around kissing baby-sitters." Grace smiled, pleased with herself. "I believe we're making progress."

IT WAS ODD, he realized, walking through his empty house. So strange to be in his home without the girls. Without his sister or brother-in-law or his nieces, the old place sure felt empty. And so did he. Owen remembered to put the bouquet of flowers from the bar in a jug of water, and then he poured himself a jigger of brandy and sat down in his favorite chair, an old green leather one that had seen better days, just as the house had. Just as Owen's heart had. Sometimes he thought about building something new, but the old, two-story farm house was solid, still in good shape, with plenty of room for a growing family. He'd planned to build his own place and give his sister, Judy, and her husband the house, but there hadn't been time.

In a matter of months, everything had changed. Life was like that. A few days ago he'd walked into the Bliss ladies' house and seen a woman he wanted more than he'd ever wanted anyone in his life.

And tonight she was taking care of Melanie and he had no doubt she would do a good job of it, too. But he should have put them both—baby and woman— into his truck and brought them home, put Mel in her crib and Suzanne in his bed.

Where they belonged.

"THERE, THERE, SWEETHEART," Suzanne murmured, rocking the baby in her arms. Mrs. Whitlow's oak rocking chair had come in handy at four o'clock this morning, when Melanie's cries began. So Suzanne changed her diaper, fed her a bottle and rocked her until she fell asleep once again. Melanie's whimpers stopped and all Suzanne could hear was the faint sound of the child's steady breathing and the creak of the rocker when it hit a certain place on the wood floor.

From the window Suzanne could see the rooftops and windows of other Bliss homes. The streetlights illuminated sidewalks and crossroads, but she had noticed only one car pass by. She saw a light on in a house across the street and wondered if another woman was awake and caring for a child.

Suzanne was in no hurry to put the baby back in her crib. She'd pay for the lack of sleep later on in the day, but for now she enjoyed the unusual peace that came from comforting a child into a restful sleep. If she'd married six months ago, she might be pregnant now. No, Suzanne told herself, they had decided to wait five years. She couldn't remember why, except that Greg thought marriage would be a big enough change without adding more.

She wondered what he would have done if he'd inherited the responsibility of two nieces. He wouldn't have taken to fatherhood well, especially if he had to care for them by himself.

Unlike Owen, Suzanne decided, Greg would have

been pretty ticked. She wondered what she ever saw in the man—beyond the charm. She'd been blinded by that sexy smile for more months than she wanted to remember. And here she was, happily rocking a baby, thinking about marriage and children and a rancher with dark brown eyes and a stubborn goodness that made him take care of what was his.

Falling in love—or falling in lust—with Owen Chase was completely out of the question, and she was suddenly very afraid she'd fall under the Bliss spell and end up barefoot, pregnant and cleaning out a barn.

And what made matters worse, she hated wearing shoes, had a secret longing for children, and had spent every summer from age six to seventeen at a horse camp.

Suzanne knew she was in trouble. There was only one thing to do, and that was to get out of town before she really and truly fell in love with a cowboy.

"SEE FOR YOURSELF," Louisa said, parking their car in front of the inn. "That's all I ask."

"Ha" was the only response Ella could come up with. She didn't mind stopping to see Grace after church, and she certainly didn't mind seeing what kind of guests the inn had this weekend. She did feel a little left out of things, though, if the truth be told.

"Grace said the girl was very maternal," Louisa

added. "She stayed with Owen's baby all night and did just fine. Grace thinks she enjoyed herself, too. And Owen is going to come pick up the child soon, so we'll see them together again."

"I thought you'd grown tired of matchmaking," Ella grumbled. She liked being the oldest; she liked being in charge. All of a sudden Louisa was upsetting everything, and Ella didn't like it. "I thought you wanted to find a man for yourself, which, by the way, I still find ridiculous."

"Several possibilities appeared last night," her sister said, as she shut off the car engine and placed the keys in her purse. Louisa liked to drive the car, while Ella preferred to sit in the passenger seat and give directions. Louisa used to be so good at taking directions.

"How old were these 'possibilities,' Louisa? Anyone under the age of ninety?"

"I'm not telling," she said, and opened her car door. "Are you coming inside or not?"

"I'm coming," Ella grumbled. But in fact she looked forward to visiting with Grace and discussing last night's dance. "I saw some interesting women for Calder Brown last night, if he shows up in town soon. And then there's Gabe, who I feel might be hopeless."

"Let's get Owen settled first, dear," her sister said, as they hooked arms and traveled carefully along the snowy path to Grace's front door. "And then me. Do you think Pete Peterson is too young for me?"

"Yes."

"Oh."

"Sister, there aren't many men in town who *aren't* too young for you. A bitter pill to swallow, I know, but there you are."

"Reality bites."

"What?"

"Never mind," Louisa said, sighing. "Just something I heard on television." She knocked on the front door, which opened almost immediately.

Grace stood back to let them enter. "Come on in, ladies," she said, waving them inside. "And hurry. Our reporter is packing to go back to New York."

"IT'S TIME, REALLY. I'm sure I have enough material for the story," Suzanne told the three women. She hated disappointing them, but she wasn't sure she could resist Owen *and* his baby. And she wasn't going to admit she'd fallen just a little bit in love with both of them. The ladies would swoon with delight over that news. "Did I tell you I saw a wedding last night? I think I got some great pictures."

"But you can't leave now," Louisa insisted, her teacup rattling in its saucer. The women had arranged themselves around the dining room table as if having a war council. Melanie sat in her high chair and banged plastic measuring cups together while Suzanne, packed and ready to run, waited for Grace to add up her bill.

Ella frowned at her. "What about Owen Chase?"

Suzanne pretended to misunderstand. "He didn't want to be in my story, anyway. I'm sure he'll be relieved."

Grace threw up her hands. "I'm too upset to add these figures." She shoved the papers toward Ella. "You do it, Ella. You were always good with numbers."

"Oh, for heaven's sake," the elder Bliss sister grumbled. She picked up a pencil and began tallying.

Louisa looked as if she wanted to cry. "Aren't you going to say goodbye to him?"

"Of course I am," Suzanne fibbed. She'd actually hoped to get an earlier start than this, but Melanie had changed that particular plan. Every time Suzanne left the room, the child cried. And when she returned, Mel would lift her arms to be held. Even now Suzanne stood near the high chair, because every few minutes the child would look over and smile, as if she was relieved to see her so close. "He should be here any minute now." She looked at her watch. "Did he tell us what time he was coming?"

"After chores," Grace said. "You never know,

though. There are a lot of chores to do on a ranch. And Owen is a hard worker."

"Yes," Louisa said. "A fine man and a hard worker. A girl couldn't do better."

"You can stop matchmaking now," Suzanne told them. "I really do have to go home."

"But why?" Ella held up the reservations form. "It says here you were planning to stay another week."

"And we're supposed to get more snow," Louisa said. "And the first quilt raffle is tonight. You did buy a ticket, didn't you?"

"Two of them, but—"

"You could get lucky," Louisa insisted. "There are other prizes, too, you know. Dinner for two at some of our fine restaurants. The new bakery is giving away a free wedding cake."

"Calder chipped in a side of beef," Ella added. "And Owen—what did Owen contribute this year?" She frowned, trying to remember.

"It doesn't matter," Suzanne said. "Really, it doesn't." She picked up her purse, stacked on top of her luggage, and dug through it until she found the raffle ticket button. "There," she declared, laying it on the table. "You can decide who gets what."

"Oh, dear," Louisa said, looking at the baby. Mel must have thought Suzanne was going to leave, for she put her arms up and wailed. "There she goes again."

The doorbell rang, so Grace stood up and headed toward the foyer. "That might be Missy. I called her and told her to—oh, come on in."

A man's voice greeted Grace, and Suzanne knew exactly who that voice belonged to. She could have been out of here without having to say goodbye if she'd been able to leave when she'd first tried to. She hated goodbyes, especially when she didn't really want to go. No, she told herself, straightening her shoulders and preparing to look professional. She wasn't thinking about love and romance and making love to a dark-eyed rancher. She *was* getting out of this crazy town before its spell trapped her completely.

Melanie continued to wail, and Suzanne couldn't bear it any longer. She moved the plastic tray and lifted the baby into her arms once again. Melanie hiccuped against her neck and relaxed, her little feet dangling against Suzanne's hip, so when Owen walked into the dining room he looked relieved at the sight of the baby in her arms.

"Good morning, ladies," he said, with that slight smile that made Suzanne wish they were alone and not wearing clothes. He took in the older women's glum expressions and then looked back at Suzanne. "What's wrong?"

"Nothing," she assured him. "Melanie is a little fussy this morning and just likes being held, that's all." She turned so the baby could see her uncle. "See? No more tears."

"Hi, honey," he said, stepping closer to stroke her head. "You look tired."

"Her or me?" Suzanne asked, trying to sound cheerful.

"Her," he said. His hand briefly touched Suzanne's shoulder.

"We are not having a good morning," Louisa announced, causing Owen to look over to the ladies seated around the table. Grace stood at the sideboard and poured Owen a cup of coffee.

"Suzanne is leaving early," she said. "Sit down for a moment, Owen, and see if you can help us talk her out of it."

"Leaving?" He turned back to Suzanne. "What are you talking about?"

"I—I just thought, well…" Suzanne stammered.

"Well?" he asked, taking the coffee cup from Grace's outstretched hand. "What's going on?"

"She's determined to leave," Ella said. "I assume she doesn't care for Bliss."

"It's a wonderful town," Suzanne assured them, rubbing the baby's back absentmindedly. "I feel like I've fallen into Brigadoon. It just doesn't feel real."

"What a lovely movie that was," Louisa said, but Grace and Ella just shook their heads.

"Of course it's real," Ella snapped. "What kind of talk is that?"

"If Suzanne needs to leave, we've no business trying to talk her out of it," Owen said. He set his untouched coffee on the dining room table and reached for his niece. "Here, I'll take her. We need to be getting back to the ranch, anyway."

Suzanne attempted to give the child to Owen, but Melanie had a different idea. She fussed and put her head back down on Suzanne's shoulder.

"She's been like this since last night," Suzanne explained. "We spent a lot of time in the rocking chair."

"Your arms must be ready to fall off," Grace said, then looked at Owen. "That baby hasn't let Suzanne out of her sight for five minutes."

Owen tried again. This time those large hands attempted to peel the child from Suzanne in the most gentle way possible, but Melanie protested with such a high-pitched scream he had no choice but to release her.

"Sorry," Suzanne said. "Has she ever been like this before?"

"Not too often."

"Maybe she's getting into one of those stages," Grace said. "My kids did that. Would scream and holler at people they used to smile at the week before. It's just a phase," she said. "She'll get over it."

"In the meantime," Owen drawled, "what do I do?"

Ella supplied the answer. "Take Suzanne home with you, of course."

"Excuse me?"

"It's very simple," Ella told the rancher, while the others looked on with varying degrees of amazement on their faces. "Suzanne goes home with you and puts Melanie to bed in her own crib. As soon as she falls asleep, Suzanne can leave."

"We'd have to take two cars so I could leave," Suzanne said. "And Mel will cry if Owen puts her in the truck with him."

"I could put the car seat in your car," he said. "If you don't mind coming with us. What time does your plane leave?"

"Six thirty-eight. Tomorrow morning."

"Ella," Louisa said. "You are brilliant."

"Agreed," Grace declared. "This should work out beautifully."

"Wait," Suzanne said, but not very loud. Not loudly enough for anyone but Owen to hear.

"It's your call," he said. "Your decision. I can take her now and she'll cry, but she'll get over it. Once she's in the truck she'll probably fall back to sleep."

"I don't know about that," Suzanne said, stroking the child's hair. "She's not very happy this morning."

"Neither am I," he said, smiling just a little. "I wanted to show you my ranch. It's a part of Montana you might want to see."

"I can't stay," she said.

"I know. Come home with me, anyway," Owen said.

"All right." If she couldn't stay, she should at least see what she was leaving behind.

9

"WHAT DID I MISS?" Missy hopped out of her car as Suzanne drove away down Elm Street, Owen's truck in front of her leading the way north. "What kind of emergency did you have?"

"The redhead wanted to leave," Ella explained as Missy hurried up the walk toward the porch where the others stood. Ella hugged her coat closer, feeling the damp chill in the air. "We managed to delay her departure for a little while longer. How long we don't know, but at least this will give Owen a few more hours."

"Ella had such a brilliant idea to keep them together a bit longer," Louisa said. "Come on in and we'll tell you all about it"

Grace held open the door and ushered them inside, where it was warm. "Ladies, that was a close call. I thought she was going to leave any moment."

Ella looked at the overcast sky before stepping inside the house. It was going to snow and, if eighty-one years of experience was good for anything, she had a feeling it was going to be a darn good storm, too. "I think our Miss Greenway may end up staying with Owen Chase longer than she thinks. Has anyone heard a weather report?"

"Snow," Missy said. "What we had last night was just flurries. The real storm is heading our way now."

"Wonderful." Louisa clapped her hands and looked as if she wanted to dance around the room. "That baby sure helped arrange things nicely, don't you think?"

"I think I liked you better when you whined about your missing tea," Ella said. "Last week you spoke of retiring, remember? When you were in that cranky mood?"

"Life is more exciting these days," her sister said.

Missy looked intrigued. "Why? Are you still thinking about—" she lowered her voice "—the sex ship?"

"I certainly am. The hunt for a man is going quite well, in fact. I had quite a wonderful time at the dance last night."

"Oh, no," Ella moaned. "Not that again."

Grace herded them into the dining room. "Since we're all together, why don't we play a few hands of cards?"

"What about your guests?"

"Everyone has left except for the newlyweds, and

they don't come out of their room until noon," she said. "Isn't love wonderful?"

"I wouldn't know," Louisa said, giving the stairs a wistful look. "But I hope that's going to change."

OWEN KNEW DAMN WELL there was a storm coming down from the Canadian Rockies. He'd watched the Weather Channel and called Darcy to tell her he'd pick her up early, right after he got Mel. She'd begged to stay awhile longer, with Jen's mother agreeing to let her spend another night and go to school tomorrow morning. It was easy to agree to that, knowing that he'd see Suzanne today. He'd half hoped he could show her the ranch.

He knew she'd like the place, if only to photograph it for her magazine. She wouldn't have turned down a chance to see a working cattle ranch run by the bachelor at the top of the Bliss ladies' hit list.

Owen also knew he could manage Melanie all by himself, despite her screams and sniffles and fussy ways. Three weeks ago she'd pulled the same thing with Darcy, refusing to allow her sister to leave the room, and demanding to be held when anyone walked by the high chair or the playpen. Once the tooth popped through her gums she was fine, her usual cheerful self. Owen figured it would be that way again.

Suzanne didn't need to know that, though. Not

right away. He looked in the rearview mirror to see her Ford Explorer right on his tail. She'd been surprisingly good with Mel, something he hadn't expected, even though he'd seen her hold the child the first time he met her.

So maybe the Bliss ladies were right and this matchmaking thing could actually work. He'd noticed the women looked pretty pleased with themselves when he got in his truck, Suzanne and Mel settled in her car, and both engines revved up, ready to go. He had Ella Bliss to thank for this idea. He'd show Suzanne his home, which pretty much was all he had to offer. And he sure wouldn't mind the adult company for a few hours.

He'd let the woman think he needed her. It sure was the truth.

And he wouldn't mention anything about the snowstorm, either. At least not right away.

OF COURSE THE RANCH WAS perfect, picturesque to the max, though it proved impossible to take pictures while balancing a baby on her hip. Suzanne planned to try again after Melanie had gone to bed for her nap. Before she got in her car and headed for Great Falls and a motel by the airport.

The Chase Ranch stretched for miles, as far as the eye could see, in every direction. At the end of a long drive off the county road lay the "main house," as

Owen called it, and a number of outbuildings of various shapes, sizes and ages. Several horses pranced in a snow-packed corral, their attention focused on Owen as he approached the fence.

"Do you ride?" he asked.

"Actually I do."

He looked surprised. "I wouldn't have guessed that."

"I spent my summers at horse camp," Suzanne explained. "After my parents died, my aunt and uncle tried to find things to keep me busy."

"Did you mind?"

"I loved it." She leaned on the railing and let Mel get a closer look at the horses. The child didn't seem to notice the cold; her little pink hat covered her ears and the sleeves of her matching jacket folded over to cover her tiny hands. "What about Darcy? Does she like living out here?"

"It's always been her home," Owen said. "Sometimes I think about finding a place to live in town so Darcy could be near her friends and school—I could come out here to work each day—but Darcy won't hear of it. She's had enough changes to deal with as it is, I guess, so I figure she'll let me know when something's wrong."

"She must love you very much."

He shrugged. "I don't know much about raising girls, but I do my best."

"I'm sure you do." He was a man who did his duty and kept his promises. Even if that meant taking care of two children who weren't his.

Owen turned away from the horses. "Come on inside and I'll show you the house."

"Can I take pictures?" She could at least pretend she was still working. It was a good defense against the memory of last night's embrace and the tension that lay between them now.

"Do whatever you like." He reached over and plucked Melanie from Suzanne's arms, and the child never uttered a sound of protest. She grinned and grabbed Owen's nose instead. "But let's get out of the cold."

"You little stinker." Suzanne laughed at the baby's silly expression. "You've been faking all along."

"She's temperamental like that," her uncle explained. "She gets something in her head and then won't stop. She might want you—and only you— again when she's ready for a nap."

Suzanne hid a yawn. They were close to the house now, a sturdy two-story white Victorian with several unusual additions tacked on. She followed Owen to the back porch, a wide cement rectangle that overlooked the outbuildings and the largest barn.

"I'm sorry she kept you awake last night," he said, reaching for his keys. He unlocked the back door and opened it so she could step inside. "Watch out. This is the mud room, so don't trip over any boots or tools."

When he flicked on the overhead light, Suzanne saw what Owen meant. The mud room looked like a good place to hold everything dirty that Owen didn't want in the rest of the house. There was even a saddle in the corner and some ropes hanging from a hook near a tall cupboard. Despite Owen's warnings, an array of work boots were lined up neatly along one wall, and the only tools she saw were hanging on another wall above a long bench.

"Should I take off my shoes?"

"That depends on how long you're staying." He gave her a quick smile. "Do you want to make yourself comfortable and see the house, or do you want to take a few pictures outside and get on the road? If you want to stay, I can make coffee. And we can attempt to get Mel to take a nap." The baby patted his face and squealed as if she recognized the word.

"All right," Suzanne agreed, though she knew she'd be better off getting back in her car and heading out of here. She had no business being here, not really. Owen Chase was a man looking for a long-term relationship. Looking—whether he admitted it or not—for a wife, and a mother for his children. She wasn't that woman.

She had a great job, a healthy trust fund and a broken heart. She had no business lusting after a Montana rancher with more responsibilities than any man she'd ever met. She had no reason to want to stay in Bliss, no matter how much fun the place was during festival season. She didn't believe in matchmaking and she didn't want to get married.

And she didn't want to tell herself the truth, either, so Suzanne hung her jacket on a hook by the door, kicked off her boots and followed Owen into the kitchen.

"DO YOU REALLY THINK this will work?" Suzanne stood next to Owen in Melanie's pink-and-white bedroom as they watched the baby fuss in her crib. Those dark eyes held tears and her mouth puckered into a frown as she stared at the adults on the other side of the wooden slats. "She doesn't look very sleepy."

"She only fusses when she's tired or she's getting a tooth," he explained. "Don't be surprised when she starts yelling at us."

Suzanne patted the baby and stifled another yawn. Even a cup of Owen's strong coffee hadn't given her the jolt of energy she needed to stay awake. She adjusted the blanket over the child. "I'll stay with her awhile, just to make sure she's okay."

"She'll be asleep in five minutes," he predicted. "I'll go fix something for lunch."

"Okay." So this was what happened when the biological clock started ticking. A perfectly self-reliant, independent and emotionally stable woman was reduced to wanting nothing more than to rock a baby to sleep. Right now Melanie seemed content to settle for having her tummy rubbed, though she babbled softly to herself and made sure that Suzanne stayed with her.

Gradually Suzanne stopped rubbing and lifted her hand away from the baby, whose eyes immediately flew open.

"I'm right here," Suzanne assured her. She sat down on the edge of the double bed three feet away from the crib and imagined Owen's sister sleeping here when she was a girl. The room was decorated in faded pink-and-yellow rose wallpaper, lacy curtains and white-painted furniture.

Melanie didn't close her eyes immediately, so Suzanne lay on the soft, puffy yellow comforter, her head on a thick pillow, and faced the baby so that they were almost at eye level. "See? I'm going to go to sleep with you." She'd seen her sisters do the same thing with their babies, but Suzanne hadn't realized just how tired they must have been after spending a long night trying to comfort a child.

After Melanie relaxed and closed her eyes, so did Suzanne. Just for a minute, she promised herself. Just for a few blissful moments she would shut her eyes and rest. Then she would have lunch with Owen and bid him a very civilized goodbye.

She snuggled into the pillows and thought about the past hour. Owen had given her a tour of the first floor of his home, a solid, comfortable house that was surprisingly clean. She wondered if he hired someone to come in and do the housework. The floors were pine, the walls ivory, and at the end of the large living room was a fieldstone fireplace and a man-size leather recliner. The furniture was old and brown and comfortable looking; family photographs decorated the walls, and leaf-patterned, bark cloth drapes hung in front of the tall windows on two sides of the room.

Suzanne thought she heard the wind batter the windows, but she didn't open her eyes. Instead she fell asleep and dreamed of elderly ladies waving goodbye as she wore a white gown and rode a rugged quarter horse toward Owen Chase.

OWEN HAD BEEN TOLD the rule: never wake a sleeping baby. And he'd learned the hard way that that particular advice should be followed whenever possible.

But what about a sleeping woman? One who intended to drive to Great Falls. One who didn't know a storm had begun, with snow falling furiously out of a heavy gray sky. She shouldn't—couldn't—drive off in a storm, so why not let her sleep?

There lay the dilemma, and Owen stood in the doorway of Melanie's room and wondered which way to go. Whatever would make Suzanne less angry with him would be best, he figured, so he opted to do nothing. Let the woman sleep. He would put the sandwiches in the refrigerator and go out and get the chores done before the weather got too bad.

If he was more like Calder, he would have no scruples about seducing the woman. Calder would tell him that fate had given him a snowstorm and a beautiful woman in one of his beds, so what was he waiting for? Gabe would tell him the same thing, but Gabe and Calder were handsome men, used to getting their way with females since they'd all been in fifth grade together. Owen was the shy one, the one who'd stood on the sidelines years later at teenage parties, his hands in his pockets, unable to speak to girls without blushing and stammering.

Some things never changed.

But before he went downstairs again, Owen went into his bedroom and took a worn quilt off his bed. He thought Suzanne might be cold, and he didn't think she would wake if he was very careful and very quiet when he spread it over her. And she didn't. Not really.

He thought she might have smiled a little, though,

which made him long to lift a tendril of hair from her cheek. But he didn't. He would let her sleep for as long as she needed to, and then he would help her get to Great Falls in time for tomorrow's flight.

He had moved away when he heard her whisper. "Owen?"

He turned. "Yes."

She blinked, looking sleepy and confused and very beautiful. "I must have fallen asleep."

"It's allowed." He glanced over at Melanie, to see her still sleeping soundly, then stepped closer to the bed.

"How long have I been up here?"

"About an hour, that's all."

"What time is it?"

"Close to three. Mel's still asleep," he said, keeping his voice low.

"Oh, good." Suzanne smiled, and this time he reached over and swept the hair from her cheek and tucked it behind her ear. Her skin was like satin under his roughened fingers. She didn't seem to mind his touch.

"You don't have to get up," he said. "You can go back to sleep if you want."

"I'm not a very good guest. And I missed lunch."

"It'll keep." He sat carefully on the edge of the bed, in the space made by the indentation of her waist. "Look, Suzanne, there's something you should know."

"You have three wives, six illegitimate children and this really isn't your ranch?"

"What?"

"Sorry." Once again she gave him that sleepy smile that turned his heart upside down. "Wishful thinking."

"Maybe you should go back to sleep."

Suzanne shook her head. "What was it you wanted to tell me?"

"It's snowing."

"Snowing." She didn't seem to understand the significance of his weather report.

"It's snowing a *lot*. And it's going to keep on snowing. We get these storms from the Canada—"

"And we're snowed in?" She rolled over on her back and looked toward the window, but the curtains hid the wintery scene outside.

"No, but do you hear the wind? It's not a good idea to drive to Great Falls in a storm."

"I have four-wheel drive."

"You could have a tank, honey, but if you can't see where you're going, you could drive off the road."

"You called me 'honey.'"

"Well, you're in my bed."

"No way. This is obviously a girl's room."

He shrugged, traced his finger along her jaw.

"This was my room when I was a kid, before Judy came home and fixed it up."

"It's a very nice room."

"Thank you." His thumb brushed across Suzanne's bottom lip before he dropped his hand from her face.

"Are you going to kiss me?"

"No."

Her eyebrows rose. "No?"

He bent over her, bracing himself with one arm near her shoulder, and brushed his lips across her temple and down, to below her ear. "No. Why would I want to do that?"

Her arms lifted and looped around his neck. "No reason," she said, her voice soft and teasing. "I guess you'd rather be outside with the cows and horses and whatever else is in all those barns."

"Sure, especially when it's snowing and the wind's howling like a freight train." Owen moved his mouth closer to her lips and, featherlight, kissed the corner of her mouth.

"And when the baby's asleep," she added.

"Yes," he said. "I love to leave the house and do chores when there's a beautiful woman in my bed." Her lips were so soft, but he didn't urge them apart. Instead he lifted his head and looked into those blue eyes and hoped like hell she wasn't going to stop smiling at him and get up.

"Your *former* bed," she said, her fingers touching his hair.

"I can show you where I sleep now," he whispered, wondering if this would be the moment she would decide to leave. "If I wasn't so anxious to go outside, that is."

"Of course. Work comes first." She pulled him toward her, but stopped short of kissing him. "This is a terrible idea."

"Just awful," he agreed, scooping her into his arms, quilt and all. "It's the worst idea I've ever had."

She rested her head on his shoulder as he carried her out of the bedroom and down the hall. His bedroom door was open, so nothing prevented him from heading straight toward his bed.

"Let me see," she said, so he turned around in a circle to show her the room. He didn't think it was anything special, probably nothing like she was used to in New York. He'd made one of the closets into a bathroom a few years ago, had new carpet installed and even bought himself a king-size bed. None of that had changed the fact that he was still alone.

"That, Owen Chase, is a very large bed."

He laid her on it and tossed the extra quilt aside. "Room for two," he said, standing beside his bed and looking down at the woman with her head on his pillow. "I bought it years ago in case some day the matchmaking festival was a personal success."

"And?"

"It was. Is. Could be. Beyond my wildest expectations."

Suzanne laughed. "Do you think the old ladies planned this?"

"If that's the case," he said, putting one hand on the brass headboard as he leaned over her, "I have new respect for Ella Bliss."

Suzanne's smile dimmed. "Owen..."

She had changed her mind about his room and his bed. The world wouldn't end. They could play Scrabble until the snow stopped and he cleared the drive to the main road. "Come on downstairs and have lunch."

He started to move away, but Suzanne reached up and touched his face. She gave him an odd look and traced his lips with her index finger. "I was only going to ask where Darcy is."

"In town until after school tomorrow."

"In that case, could we talk about kissing again?"

If he hadn't fallen in love with her yet, he did at that moment. His heart may as well have tumbled out of his chest and into her hands for safekeeping.

10

IF THIS WAS LOVE, lust, infatuation or some strange acceptance of Bliss tradition, so be it. Suzanne gave up. She no longer wanted to fight against passion or snowstorms or the matchmaking strength of four elderly, gray-haired women. Meeting Owen Chase had changed her.

She accepted her fate. At least for this afternoon. And reached for the rancher who looked at her as if he thought she might disappear at any moment.

Instead of answering her question, he lowered his mouth to hers and kissed her. Not a gentle brushing of the lips this time; the kiss drove thoughts of snow and matchmaking completely out of her head. She reached for him, ran her hands up his chest and tugged on the front of his shirt. He lowered himself onto the bed, following her down into the nest of pillows tossed against the headboard.

He braced himself above her with his powerful arms, the long length of his body stretched taut along hers. She would have moved her legs to cradle him against the aching need between her thighs, but she was pinned beneath him. His arousal was evident, even through the thick denim of his jeans, and she wanted nothing more than to take him inside of her.

His tongue moved in erotic patterns inside of her mouth, making her yearn for more. Her fingers moved against his face, into his hair, urging him closer, until he withdrew and lifted his mouth from hers.

Owen shifted his large body to the side, drawing her with him so they were face-to-face, body-to-body, and he was free to caress her. He slipped his hand under the hem of her sweater and stroked her heated skin until her breast swelled against his palm. Somehow he managed to remove her sweater, lifting it carefully over her head in a slow motion that only added to this surprising, aching need she felt for him, to take him within her.

"Wait," she said, not wanting to wait at all; rather, she wanted to feel more of him. Owen unhooked the center clasp of her bra, baring her breasts to the cool air before he stopped, his large hand splayed across her rib cage.

"Suzanne?"

"Your shirt." She reached for the buttons with trembling fingers and managed to undo two before he moved her hands away and completed the job himself. Skin-to-skin, neither could wait any longer.

He unzipped her slacks; she managed to peel them off, along with her underwear, and kick the clothing to the foot of the bed. She wore nothing but her socks when he left the bed and stripped the rest of his own clothing off. She heard the wind then, the sounds of freezing snow smacking against the bedroom windows. It was the perfect afternoon to be in bed in a darkening room with a man she couldn't resist. She moved to slip off her socks, watched with relief as Owen opened the drawer of his nightstand and retrieved a condom. She'd had no use for birth control for many months and hadn't thought she'd want to make love to anyone for a long, long time.

How wrong she'd been.

Owen returned to her again, but this time when their bodies met on the mattress it was with a searing heat, a trembling touch, a kiss that promised everything each other wanted. His callused hands warmed her skin and drew her to him. He covered her, warmed her with his large body, and she moved to welcome him into her own.

She was more than ready for him, and urged his body closer until the tip of him pressed against her. He was hot and hard and soon all hers, embedded deep inside, causing an exquisite stretching sensation.

He stilled. "Are you...all right?"

She touched his cheek, glided her fingertips over his skin. "Yes. Perfect."

Owen shifted his body, moving even deeper inside of her before partially withdrawing and then filling her again. His movements were slow and controlled, as if he had all the time in the world to make love to her. Each stroke flooded her with a sweet sensation of pleasure, with the need to feel him deep inside her again and again. She suddenly knew this man could make love to her for hours or minutes or days like this and she would welcome every caress, every kiss, every sweet invasion of her body from a man who was no longer a stranger.

"Owen," she whispered, but then the orgasm she hadn't expected began to build with a dizzying intensity that took her breath away. She arched against him as he deepened his thrusts, and when she tightened and climaxed around him she felt his own control break. He stiffened, increasing the sensation flooding her, and groaned as he found his own release.

She was still trembling when Owen reached for the quilt he'd brought with them into his room. Realizing that neither one of them had the energy to rearrange themselves under the bedcovers, he tucked the quilt around them and kept Suzanne in his arms. She fell asleep with her head on his pillow and her hand on his heart.

OWEN WOKE WHEN HE HEARD Melanie's wail of hunger. He hoped it was hunger, easily remedied, rather than teething pain that was making the baby cry. He blinked and wondered where he was. At first he didn't know why the room was so dark or what time it was and whose forehead was pressed against his left arm.

And then he remembered. And smiled. And thanked all the stars in heaven for giving him this woman and this storm. And this bed. He didn't want to forget to thank the stars for the bed. That could be bad luck.

Owen knew he needed all the luck he could get, but first he wanted to get to Mel before she woke Suzanne. He disentangled himself from the sleeping woman and the quilt that covered them, but once he was out of bed he rearranged the quilt to cover Suzanne, every sweet, naked inch of her, as fast as he could.

Then he grabbed his jeans and hurried down the hall before Mel screamed the house down. Later, his jeans on and his baby in his arms, sucking down a bottle, Owen sat in his favorite chair and pondered his life. A lot had changed in the past few hours: Suzanne had visited his home and ended up in his bed. It was a pretty good turn of events.

And now he had to figure out how to get her to stay. It was almost six, dinnertime. He would thaw a couple of steaks, build a fire, open that expensive bottle of brandy Calder had given him for his birthday last year. He'd get Suzanne's bags out of her car and he'd do the outside chores in record time.

But first things first. He needed to get some baby food in Melanie and put some clean clothes on her. And he sure wouldn't mind a hot shower, either, but that would have to wait until later on, after the baby went to sleep and the chores were finished. But more than anything else he wanted to return to bed and make love to Suzanne all night.

He'd never figured himself to be a romantic man, but now he believed in love at first sight. He'd been speechless when he'd met her, and later, unable to keep from touching her. And Suzanne? He didn't know what she expected. Her life was worlds away from his, and for all he knew she would treat this interlude as nothing more than sex. What if she thought of this as only a brief encounter, a fling? Something to fill in the time while researching her article?

Owen sighed, and Melanie took the bottle out of her mouth and grinned at him.

"I'm too old for flings," he told her. "Too old and—don't take this personally, sweetheart—too lonely."

"Ba ba," Melanie gurgled, blinking at him as if she understood every word.

"Yeah, well, you're going to break some hearts yourself in about eighteen years." She hit his arm with the plastic bottle and then laughed. "Tell you what," Owen said, lifting her to a standing position on his lap. "You sleep through the night tonight and I'll buy you a pony."

"Ba," Melanie said.

"I'll take that as a yes." If this was only a snow-induced fling, he needed to make the most of every hour.

"You go do your chores and I'll do the dishes." Owen looked at her as if she'd just offered to build a new barn, so Suzanne said, "Let me guess. An offer like that doesn't come along every day?" She picked up the sponge from the edge of the sink and squeezed the water out of it.

Owen set his dirty dishes on the counter and gave her that wry smile of his. "There've been a few things happening around here lately that don't come along every day."

"I know how to do dishes," she assured him. "And I even know how to clean cereal off a baby and change diapers. Auntie Sue will take care of everything."

"I like your hair up like that." He leaned over and kissed the back of her neck. "Is Auntie Sue going to meet Uncle Owen in his bed later on?"

"If he doesn't tick her off between now and then, I think something can be arranged." She kept her voice light and teasing, her hands on the sponge, instead of turning around and going into his arms. It would be so easy to rest her forehead in the middle of his chest and make a fool of herself by bursting into tears. For some reason she felt like one quivering mass of emotions, but scaring the solid rancher wasn't necessary. She could manage to hold herself together until he went outside and she was alone.

Owen put his hands on her shoulders and turned her around to face him. "Hey," he said, lifting her chin with gentle fingers so she had to look into his eyes. "Are you okay?"

"Of course." She gave him a bright smile. "You've never seen the domestic side of me, that's all."

"I'm not talking about doing dishes," he said. "Are you okay with staying here tonight, until the storm is over?"

"I'm fine with it. Really." *Until the storm is over.*

He frowned a little and his voice softened. "I put your bags in my bedroom, but you know you can sleep in Judy's old room tonight if that's what you want."

"And what do you want, Owen?"

"You." He bent his head and kissed her. "Just you, remember?"

"Is it really that simple?" She'd only met the man

four days ago, and here she was loading his dishwasher, rocking his baby and making love to him. The thought of their time in bed together brought heat to her face.

"For now." He hesitated, as if he didn't know what to do about her.

"I'll see you later," she promised. "Go."

"Yes, ma'am." The smile he gave her threatened to make her cry again, so Suzanne turned around and busied herself by turning on the hot water and filling the sink. She had to get a grip on herself, before she did or said something she couldn't take back. In a moment she heard the door to the mud room close above the sounds of Mel's happy chattering.

It was a cozy scene. The baby seemed content to sit in her high chair and bang spoons and plastic measuring cups against the tray. Suzanne kept an eye on her as she rinsed the dishes and loaded the dishwasher. Unlike the narrow kitchen area of her own apartment, this room had plenty of counter space beneath the yellow-painted cupboards, and more storage than she could picture any one woman being able to use. The counter stretched in a large U-shape; the refrigerator was oversize and the dining table at least eight feet long. She felt at home in this large room, with the strange desire to bake bread. To *nest*, for heaven's sake.

She'd only known the man four days. She'd made

love with him once. And when she'd awakened in the dark room an hour and a half ago, she'd been disappointed that he wasn't beside her. She had reached for him, smelled him on her skin and on the pillows. She had lain in the bed for a while, listening to the wind outside and the comforting sounds of Owen downstairs—the clattering of pans, doors closing, water running. It had been one of those moments when she felt as if she was in exactly the right place at precisely the right time.

With the right man.

A hot shower and a steak dinner hadn't altered that strange feeling of belonging in a place and with a man she hadn't known five days ago. She and Owen had exchanged stories of their families, shared a bottle of wine, talked of Darcy and Mel and life in Montana. He'd explained cattle and grasslands and the history of his ranch. She'd told him of her recent vacation in Italy with two friends from college, and some of the articles she'd written for the magazine.

And now she wanted to cry, because she was in the perfect place with a man she did not want to love.

If the matchmakers could only see her now.

"It's still snowing hard. What do you think, Ella?" Louisa parted the drapes and looked out of the living room toward Elm Street. "Will the raffle be canceled?"

"I have no idea." Ella refused to put down the Sunday paper and discuss it. Louisa was only interested in chasing men these days. Trying to talk her out of it did no good.

"You're the one in charge of it, aren't you?" Louisa sighed and turned away. She ambled over to the couch and sat down beside her sister.

"Not anymore. The churches have taken turns for the past three years." She turned the page and continued reading about the current trend in running shoes. If Lou continued to whine about her social life, Ella decided she'd buy herself a fancy new pair of sneakers and run screaming into the night.

"Well, what am I supposed to do? I've made *plans*, you know."

Which meant her sister intended to gad about with every single old man in town in hopes of something romantic happening. A chilling thought, so Ella pretended she didn't hear the comment.

"It's close to seven already. How can you sit there and read the paper when we should be getting ready to go out?"

Ella lowered the paper and turned to glare at her sister. "I don't think I'm going to risk a broken hip so you can flirt with Pete Peterson and old man Cameron."

"And Hal," Louisa added.

"Hal?" Ella didn't know anybody named Hal.

"He puts gas in the car and his wife died."

Ella gave thanks that she hadn't been born with an overactive imagination. Or sex drive. Louisa must have gotten those genes, even if they had kicked in a little late to do any good. "I suppose you could call Grace and ask. She goes to St. Luke's, so she'd be the one to know."

Louisa took herself off to the kitchen, and Ella returned to her newspaper. Another earthquake in Chile and the president's new tax cuts dominated the front page, but even those subjects couldn't keep Ella's interest for long. She heard her sister chattering like a magpie, and it wasn't long before Louisa returned to the living room and plopped down in the wing chair in front of the fireplace.

"Postponed," she said. "St. Luke's furnace is giving them trouble, and aside from that, no one wants to venture out in the storm. I guess it would be different if the snow had stopped and there was time to plow the parking lot."

"Well, I'm not surprised." Ella folded the newspaper and placed it neatly in the magazine rack. "These November storms can be quite aggravating."

"And disappointing." Louisa sighed. "I was going to have so much fun."

"Look at it this way, dear," Ella said. "The storm

may have delayed your plans, but it worked out rather well for Owen Chase. I think Miss Greenway is quite taken with the man. Once she sees his lovely ranch and gets to know him, she'll think twice about leaving."

Louisa chuckled. "He'd better be showing her more than just his ranch, if you know what I mean."

"Louisa, for heaven's sake," Ella grumbled, but the thought of Owen Chase's happiness was all that mattered. And if he and the redhead were experiencing the physical aspects of marriage a little before the wedding ceremony, so be it.

The end often justified the means.

OWEN TOLD HIMSELF he would not fall in love with her any more than he already was. Passion was one thing, commitment another. Just because he knew with every beat of his heart that Suzanne Greenway was the one woman in the world for him didn't mean he was ready for wedding rings and till-death-do-them-part.

At least not tonight. Tonight was for romance, for firelight and brandy and lovemaking in the bed—instead of on top of it. For sweet, lazy foreplay and a long night where neither one of them got much sleep.

He could hardly wait. He did the chores in record time, hung his snow-covered clothes on hooks in the mud room and hurried into the kitchen. He smelled fresh-brewed coffee, but most of the dishes were still in the sink and the room was empty. He carried his boots into the living room to thaw by the fire he'd built before dinner, but Suzanne and Mel weren't in there, either. He set his boots on the stone hearth and added a couple of logs to the fire to keep it going, then headed for the stairs.

Pausing at the bottom, he heard Suzanne's voice, listened to the laughter and the splashing of water in the hall bathroom, the one Darcy used for hours on end. Owen took the steps two at a time and peered past the half-open door to see Melanie splashing in the bathtub and Suzanne kneeling on the floor, one hand on the baby's back to keep her balanced.

"Hey." Owen pushed the door open and leaned in the doorway.

"Say hi to Uncle Owen," Suzanne told the child, then turned to smile at him. "I realized this was the only way I could get all that cereal out of her hair. I hope you don't mind."

"No." It wasn't part of the romantic picture he'd painted of his evening, but he could wait. He wasn't very good at waiting—patience didn't run in the family—but he could learn. "Of course not."

She lifted the baby out of the tub and set her on a towel, then wrapped another around her. "Should I get her ready for bed?"

"Sure. Her pajamas are in the top drawer of the dresser, diapers are in boxes on the floor. You want help?"

"No, we're fine," she assured him. "Go do whatever you have to do."

"I'm going to go clean up."

She was too busy with Mel to look at him. "Take your time. We're having fun."

"Sure." He hesitated. "Sorry," he said. "I didn't ask you here to baby-sit."

Suzanne looked up and smiled at him. "So you owe me one, Mr. Chase."

"Anything. You name it."

She considered the offer, lifted the baby and stood there with Mel balanced on her hip. "I'll have to think about it."

"You do that, sweetheart, and I'll meet you downstairs in front of the fireplace in twenty minutes."

"She'll settle down that fast?"

"I promised her a pony if she'd sleep through the night."

"Good thinking." He could have sworn Suzanne blushed. "I'm impressed."

"I'm smarter than I look." Owen stepped back to let them out of the bathroom.

Suzanne paused and, raising on her toes, kissed his cheek. "I know. The matchmakers told me."

Owen would have kissed her back, but Melanie hit him in the nose.

NOTHING WENT ACCORDING TO plan. After he got out of the shower, Darcy called to make sure he was home and safe from the storm. Mel wanted to play instead of sleep. The power went off, meaning they had no running water unless he went outside and got the generator going.

But Owen found candles, and Suzanne poured brandy in their coffee mugs. They sat in front of the fire and watched the flames while the wind roared outside. The electricity flickered back on and the baby eventually fell asleep—to dream of ponies until dawn, Owen hoped—and the snow continued to fall.

Owen took his woman's hand and led her upstairs to bed. His bed. This time he remembered to turn back the covers. This time he would make it last.

They stood very close to each other in the dark. Owen slipped his hands under her sweater and smoothed them over her warm skin. "You're not going to try to drive to Great Falls tomorrow, are you?"

"No." She reached for the waistband of his jeans and undid the snap. "I think I'll stay and have breakfast with you."

He lifted the sweater over her head and tossed it to the floor, causing her long hair to tumble over her shoulders. "You can stay for lunch, too. Why hurry off?"

"No reason," she whispered, and then unzipped his jeans. The touch of her fingers made his erection painful, and it took every ounce of self-control he owned not to tumble her back on the mattress and take her immediately. "What about you?"

Owen prayed for patience. He unhooked her bra and ran the straps down her shoulders and off her arms, exposing perfect round breasts with rose-pink nubs that peaked at his touch. "I don't have anything important to do tomorrow. I think I'm going to stay in bed all day."

"Really?" Her fingers teased the waistband of his underwear, giving him no choice but to encircle her wrists and bring her hands up to his chest. "You don't want me to touch you?"

"Later," he said. "Next time. Tomorrow. Just not now."

She leaned her forehead against his chest. "Let me know when you change your mind."

"Hold still." He smoothed his hands over her slacks, released the zipper and let the pants fall to the floor. He knelt then, and she balanced herself by putting her hands on his shoulders as he slipped off her thick socks. He pushed the slacks aside, and Suzanne was clad only in a pale triangle of satin.

"Owen," she whispered. "I'm shaking."

His only answer was to slide his hands up her legs and higher, to slip his fingers under the bands of elastic. His lips tickled her navel before he dipped lower, to sweep his tongue over the satiny fabric as he eased the material from her hips.

She was wet and ready for him, but Owen could wait. Sweet and hot and all his, Suzanne trembled and cried out when his fingers found her and eased inside. He wanted her to come against his mouth. If she was going to leave him, at least he would know the taste of her on his lips and the scent of her on his skin and the sounds she made when he gave her pleasure. She would have pulled away, but he held her against him until the contractions eased, until she found her breath.

Owen stood and lifted her in his arms and laid her gently on his bed.

By morning, Suzanne would know she was loved.

11

OWEN CHASE MADE LOVE as if each time would be the last. So when Suzanne, sleepy and sated, finally awoke late Monday morning, she knew she wouldn't be traveling any farther than back to town today, though light filtered through the white curtains and she no longer heard the wind.

She could reschedule her flight to New York. She could call Grace Whitlow to see if she could have her room back for another night or two. She would attend a few more festival functions, interview a few more people looking for someone to love, and she would finish the article.

What she wouldn't do was fall in love with the man who stood in the bedroom doorway holding a mug of hot coffee.

Owen walked over to the bed and set the mug on the nightstand. "I thought you could use this."

She sat up, tucking the sheet over her breasts, and picked up the mug. "Thanks."

He went to the window and drew back the curtains, letting sunshine into the room, then stood and stared out. "The storm's over. There's some drifting, but the roads will be cleared now that the wind has stopped."

Suzanne sipped the coffee and waited. Owen had something on his mind or he wouldn't be so quiet. "Where's Mel?"

He turned away from the window and shoved his hands in his jeans. "Playing in her crib. She's been awake since six."

"So she gets the pony."

"Yeah. Best promise I ever made." He walked over to the foot of the bed. "Thank you for last night, for staying."

Suzanne took another sip of coffee, stalling for time until she knew what to say. "It was very special."

"I wish I could ask you to stay, but I can't. Darcy—"

"I know. Uncle Owen should not have ladies spend the night." Suzanne told herself she was foolish to fall in love, and she refused to do it, but she wondered if she'd really ever had a choice. "This was just between us, and no one else needs to know...or be involved."

Owen sat down on the bed and caressed the mound of blankets that covered her foot. "Sweetheart, practically the whole town is involved."

The silly festival. Of course. "I forgot about that. I won't tell anyone if you won't."

"Just tell me you've changed your mind about leaving today."

"Owen, you need a wife, not an affair." The second the words were out she regretted them. "I'm sorry. That's none of my business."

His eyebrows rose and those dark eyes twinkled. "Are you asking me to marry you?"

"No, of course not." Flustered, she spilled some coffee on the comforter. "Oh, darn."

"I'll get you something." He went into the bathroom and came back with a hand towel. "Did you burn yourself?"

"No, I'm fine. I just made a mess, that's..." The sheet slipped when Owen sat beside her and brushed the drops of coffee from the comforter covering her lap. His arm brushed her bare breast, she felt a tingling sensation echo between her legs. The feeling increased when he bent his head and licked her hardened nipple.

"Owen," she breathed, and closed her eyes for just a moment.

"Shh," he said. She felt him lift the coffee cup from her hand and the sheet from her naked body before his lips began to trail kisses between her breasts, and lower. "When you're gone," he murmured, his breath warm upon her abdomen, "I want to remember how you taste."

MUCH LATER, when she had showered and dressed and made the necessary phone calls, Suzanne stood in the kitchen and had absolutely no idea of how to say goodbye. How did a perfectly sane, responsible and independent woman end up falling in love with a rancher in Montana? In five days, no less. And after having made love with the man more times than she could remember without blushing.

"I shoveled out your car," he said. "And the drive's plowed."

"When—?"

"This morning. I couldn't sleep," he confessed. "I kept wanting to wake you up, so I shoveled snow instead."

"I have to go."

"Are you sure you don't want lunch first?"

Her stomach was too knotted to consider food. "No, but thanks, anyway. I should get going."

"But you're staying in Bliss tonight," he stated.

"Yes. I called Mrs. Whitlow and she still has my room open."

"And then what?"

"I go home." Suzanne held his gaze for a long moment and wondered if there was anything left to say.

They lived worlds apart. This was just one of those crazy things, like the song said.

"Will you have dinner with us tonight? I have to get Darcy from school at four-thirty. We could pick you up, feed you greasy french fries and apple pie."

"You know the way to my heart."

"Not really," he said, "but I'm learning."

I will not love him, she chanted mentally all the way back to Bliss. *I will not confuse love with lust. Or pretend there is anything more to this than sexual attraction and physical needs, the cowboy mystique combined with a strange wedding phenomena in the middle of Montana.*

Her throat was sore by the time she reached town, so the first thing she did was head for the Bliss Bar and Grill. She drank a frozen margarita, ate a bag of potato chips and told herself she would get over this once she got out of this crazy town.

"SHE'S BACK," Grace whispered. "Tucked into her room as nice as can be."

Ella moved the phone closer to her ear. "Grace? Is that you?"

"Well, of course it is," she said, her voice louder now. "Can't you hear me?"

"I can now. Are you whispering for any particular reason?"

"I didn't want anyone to overhear." Grace

sounded a little miffed, so Ella attempted to switch the conversation back to its original topic.

"So our Miss Greenway has returned. Did she say anything?"

"Only that she was going to finish her research for her article tomorrow and take a few more pictures. She wants me to pose in the dining room with a few of the guests. Isn't that nice?"

Louisa hurried into the kitchen. "You're talking about Suzanne. Is she back?"

"Very nice. Just a minute, Grace." Ella supplied her sister with an update and then turned her attention back to the phone. "Did she mention Owen?"

"No, except she said she was going to take a nap, and asked if I would knock on her door at four o'clock. What do you suppose that means?"

"It means she has plans for the evening. Dinner, perhaps." Ella studied the brochure pinned to the bulletin board next to the phone. "The movie theater is hosting a free classic romance triple feature tonight. It starts at seven."

"Count me out," Louisa called, her head in the refrigerator. "I have a date."

Ella ignored her. "I can't imagine Owen Chase sitting through six hours of Cary Grant. Not on a weeknight, anyway."

"I suppose not, but I am looking forward to it myself," Grace admitted. "Missy and I are going early to get decent seats. Shall I save one for you?"

"Please," Ella said, but her mind was on the rancher's romance instead of Hollywood classics. "See if you can find out if she's seeing him tonight."

"It all sounds very promising, don't you think?"

"I do indeed." She watched her sister fix a bowl of cottage cheese and canned pineapple chunks. "It would be nice to wrap this up so we could move on to the next needy bachelor."

"Amen," Louisa said. "I have a few in mind for myself."

Ella rolled her eyes and prayed for patience. It was so much easier to assist others than to deal with one's family.

"Is THIS A DATE, Uncle Owen?" Darcy rearranged her backpack and two overstuffed duffel bags on the truck floor and then fastened her seat belt. "If it's a date, Mel and I can sit at another table."

"No way. You're sitting with me, Darce." He waved to Gabe as he drove through the school parking lot, then headed along School Street to the center of town. It was a date, all right. A date with a woman he'd fallen in love with. Trouble was, he still didn't know what in hell to do about it.

"She's beautiful."

"Yes."

"Do you think that's her real hair color?"

"I guess." Owen flushed. He knew damn well it was, and just the thought of Suzanne's naked body made him hard. He took a couple of deep breaths and shifted in his seat. "Why?"

"It's pretty. I wish my hair wasn't brown. Brown's boring."

"No it's not."

"I'm thinking about streaking it."

Owen wasn't exactly sure what Darcy was talking about, but whatever it was sounded a little suspicious. "You're fine just the way you are."

Darcy sighed.

"How was school?" He pulled onto Elm Street and drove slowly, hoping to find a parking spot near Grace Whitlow's home.

"Okay."

"And basketball?"

"Fine."

"Did you and Jen get your project finished?"

"I did the essay and she did the diagrams. It looked pretty cool. Her mom made doughnuts. *Real* doughnuts, the kind that puff up when they cook."

"Your grandmother used to make doughnuts," he told her. "Your mother and I thought that was the biggest treat in the whole world." He hadn't thought about that in years, but he could see the happy expression on Judy's face as clearly as if it was yesterday.

"You did?"

"Sure."

"Jen's mom gave me the recipe. I could make them for us."

"I'd like that." He pulled alongside the curb in a space a block past Blissful Nights B and B and shut off the engine. "Grandma's cookbooks are still around. You might even find—" He stopped, surprised to see his niece hunched over, her shoulders shaking as she held her hands to her face. "Darcy? What's the matter?"

"Nothing."

He undid his seat belt and leaned over to take her in his arms. "I'm sorry, honey."

She sobbed against his shoulder the way she had at her mother's funeral. Owen didn't know what else to do but hold her and wait for the worst to be over. Melanie babbled from the back seat, her voice growing louder as her uncle and sister didn't respond.

Darcy quieted in his embrace and sniffed loudly. "Mel's going to get mad if we don't pick her up."

"She'll be fine for a few more minutes. You want to tell me what's going on?"

Darcy sat up and wiped her face with her hands until Owen handed her a handkerchief from his jacket pocket. She blew her nose. "I get lonesome for Mom. I'm sorry."

"For what?"

"For being a pain."

"Darce." She wouldn't look at him, so he tugged on the sleeve of her jacket until she did. "You're not a pain." She gave him a look that said she didn't believe him for a minute, but she tried to smile, anyway.

"You're going to be late for your date," she said softly.

"That doesn't matter." All that mattered at the moment was making Darcy feel better, but there wasn't much he could do when they both missed her mother so much. "I'm going in to get Suzanne. You want to wait here with Mel or do you want to come in?"

"We'll wait, Uncle Owen. I'll put my stuff in the back so she has room."

Owen got out of the truck and walked down the shoveled sidewalk. This wasn't a very good start to what he'd hoped would be the perfect evening. But he'd thought he'd let Suzanne see what she was getting into, that life with him wouldn't be all-night-long sex and brandy in front of the fire. Babies cried and teenagers cried and hell, even *he* felt like crying sometimes.

Like now. When he wanted nothing more than to

take the woman home to bed, and yet he knew that this might be the last time he'd ever see her.

SHE DIDN'T WANT TO THINK about leaving tomorrow, but it was time to go, before leaving became more difficult than it already was. The town had surprised her. Main Street, with its friendly restaurants, array of stores and even a European bakery, was fun to explore. The people, despite their matchmaking fervor, were talkative and kind. But after tonight there would be nothing left to say to Owen. They'd had one night together and that was all there was to that. As happy as she would be to see him, Suzanne wished he'd never offered a goodbye dinner.

Grace Whitlow tittered and fussed when Owen entered the foyer, but Suzanne pretended his arrival was nothing out of the ordinary.

"One last interview," she told her hostess. "I won't be late."

Grace couldn't hide her disappointment. "And where are the children tonight?"

"Waiting for us," Owen said, putting a casual arm around Suzanne's shoulders. "We're going to Sam's for hamburgers."

"Well, then," Grace said, brightening a little. "You two have a good time."

Once outside on the porch, it was all Suzanne could do not to turn and kiss that sensual mouth of his. He dropped his arm from around her and took her hand, but he didn't say a word. She took a deep breath of cold air and noticed that the sky had grown dark, another early winter night in Montana.

"I should warn you," he said, when they approached the truck. He dipped his head and kept his mouth close to her ear. "Darcy's having a rough time of it tonight."

"Is there anything I can do?"

"Pretend you don't notice," was all he had time to say before the truck door opened and Darcy hopped out. Poor Darcy had puffy red eyes and looked as if she'd spent the last hour crying.

"Hi," she said, trying to smile.

"Hi," Suzanne said, walking over to the door. She wished there was something she could say or do to take that embarrassed look off the teenager's face, but she knew saying anything would just make the situation worse. Darcy moved the seat forward and climbed in the back. "Are you sure you have enough room?"

"It's okay." Darcy moved the seat back into position, and Suzanne heard Melanie screech with what sounded like delight. Suzanne climbed in the front seat, Owen shut the door and they were on their way: a silent rancher, a pathetic writer, a grieving teenager and a squealing toddler, off to the last supper.

MELANIE FUSSED, unhappy with the high chair and the strangers who smiled at her as they walked by. She pouted at her uncle and reached her hands toward Suzanne to be picked up.

"I think she wants french fries," her sister said.

"Let me take her," Suzanne said. "Maybe she's tired and just wants to be held."

"You haven't finished your dinner," Owen said.

"Neither have you." She scooted out of the booth and lifted Mel out of the high chair. The baby wrapped her arms around her neck and put her head on Suzanne's shoulder. "I guess she's tired."

"Do you really live in New York City?" Darcy pushed her half-eaten plate of food aside and rested her head on her fist. "Have you ever seen any television stars?"

Suzanne sat down, the baby against her chest. "I interviewed Martha Stewart once. Does that count?"

"I guess." She played with her straw. "Do you like Bliss?"

"Very much."

"But you're leaving."

"Yes." Suzanne patted the baby's back and avoided looking at Owen. She was afraid she'd cry and embarrass herself. "But I've had a wonderful time here."

Darcy looked down into her milk shake and didn't utter another word until later, when Owen parked the truck in front of the B and B. Before she left the truck, Suzanne turned around to say goodbye.

"Bye," the teenager whispered, since Melanie had fallen asleep the minute they left the restaurant. "I hope you come back again sometime."

"Thanks. It was really nice meeting you."

"I'll leave the engine running," Owen said. "I'll be back in a minute."

Once again he walked Suzanne up the stairs to the porch. The light was on, so he led her out of the pool of light, where they couldn't be so easily seen, and took her face between his large hands.

"I'm not going to kiss you," he said. "I'm not sure I could stop if I did."

"I know." She took a step forward and leaned against him, so he dropped his arms around her and held her to him for a long moment until Suzanne knew she had to move away. "You'd better go," she said, stepping out of his embrace.

"This isn't right." He kept his hands on her shoulders.

Suzanne took a deep breath and looked up at him. "We both knew it was only going to be for one night."

"But should it be?"

"What do you mean?"

"Stay." One word. One command. As if it was that easy.

"I can't. I have to get back to work and—"

"Marry me," he said, looking for all the world as if he knew what he was saying. Suzanne was stunned speechless, so he repeated the words. "Marry me, Suzanne."

"We've only known each other a few days," she managed to say, despite the surprising relief flooding her body.

"How long do you want?"

Good question. "I don't know."

"Do you love me?"

"Yes." And every quivering romantic inch of her wanted to fling sanity aside and agree to this crazy idea.

"And I love you. Very much."

"I think this matchmaking business has gone to your head," she said, trying to make him smile. Trying to make him stop this before she was too tempted to agree.

"Tell me that what we had—have—isn't something out of the ordinary, Suzanne. Tell me that deep in that heart of yours you don't want to stay here, with me. Tell me and I'll kiss you goodbye and walk away."

She reached up and caressed the side of his face. His skin was cool under her fingertips, but even the simple act of touching him made it impossible to say the words he'd dared her to speak. "You know I can't, Owen. But this is still crazy."

His hand closed over hers and he moved it to his lips before kissing her palm. "Not in Montana." And he smiled, held her hand to his chest. "Tomorrow we are going to go to the justice of the peace and get married."

"It's that simple?"

"During festival week it is. I'll pick you up at quarter of eight."

"In the morning?"

"It's first come, first served at the town hall. Special festival hours."

"And if I change my mind?" If she stayed awake all night and tried to talk some sense into herself and went to Great Falls instead of the town hall? "Or what if you do?"

"Then that's that. No hard feelings. No regrets."

"Just like that? No embarrassing goodbyes?"

"If that's what you want."

"So I meet you at the town hall. *If* I decide to come. *If* you decide to come."

"I'll be there," he promised. "At eight."

"If you change your mind—"

"I won't."

"You might," she said, and glanced over to his truck. "You need to go."

"Yes." He moved away and headed toward the

stairs, but when he reached the sidewalk he turned. "You're getting a package deal, you know," he said. "I promised my sister I'd take good care of them."

"I understand." Having lost her parents when she was ten, she knew what Owen's girls were going to experience. It broke her heart to think about it.

Owen looked as if there was more he wanted to say, but instead he turned toward the truck, leaving Suzanne standing in a pool of lamplight. She shivered in the cold, put her hands in her pockets and watched him get in his truck and drive away.

And now she had to get ready for a wedding.

If that was what she wanted.

12

SHE COULDN'T WEAR BLACK to her own wedding. And she wouldn't have wanted a traditional wedding gown, either, even if Cinderella's Bridal Shop was open at dawn. After last winter's fiasco she'd decided that wedding dresses could bring bad luck. Telling any of her family would be bad luck, too, Suzanne thought. She'd call everyone after she said "I do." There'd be plenty of time for family gatherings later on. She could picture her nieces worshipping Darcy and entertaining Mel. There could be a Christmas holiday on the ranch, or a delayed honeymoon in Connecticut with the family.

They would love Owen. Who wouldn't? But now her problem was finding something suitable to wear. And Grace Whitlow was her only hope.

When Suzanne knocked on the door frame of the kitchen, Grace turned away from her muffin making and smiled.

"Come on in, dear," she said. "You're a little early for muffins, but there's coffee. Look out the window. It's snowing again."

"Thanks." Suzanne helped herself from the carafe on the counter and obediently peered out of the kitchen window to see fat snowflakes drifting past. At six-thirty, she and her hostess were the only two people in the house who weren't asleep, which was convenient. "I have a favor to ask you."

"All right." Grace continued to spoon globs of muffin mix into the muffin pan.

"It might seem a little odd," Suzanne said. "But I don't know what else to do and I'm running out of time." She watched as the woman put the pan into the oven and set the timer. "Do you have a blouse I could borrow? I think we might be the same size, even though I'm taller than you."

Grace chuckled and wiped her hands on a towel. "I haven't been your size in twenty years, but I haven't thrown any clothes away in *forty* years, so you're in luck. What kind of blouse do you need?"

"Something elegant. All I have with me are sweaters, and I don't want to wear black." Suzanne hesitated and then decided she'd better explain. "Owen Chase has asked me to marry him. We're to meet at the town hall this morning." She watched Mrs. Whitlow's expression as she absorbed the information. The woman looked positively rapturous.

"Oh, my," was all she could say for a few moments. And then, after she sat down in one of her kitchen chairs, she asked, "When did this all happen?"

Suzanne joined her at the small wooden table. "Last night. We agreed to meet at the town hall—unless either one of us changes his—her—mind."

"Owen Chase doesn't change his mind," the woman said. "He must be very much in love."

"The whole thing is crazy," Suzanne confessed, trying to contain the happiness that threatened to make her cry. "But it feels so right. I can't explain it."

"Do you love him?"

"Very much."

"Then as soon as these muffins are done, we'll go upstairs to my closets. I may even have some dresses that have come round in style again." Grace beamed. "We'll find 'something borrowed' and 'something old' for good luck, too."

"Thank you," Suzanne said, feeling scared and thrilled at the same time. "Thank you for everything."

ELLA TOOK HER MORNING coffee to the table and prepared to browse through the latest issue of *Romantic Living* magazine, but Louisa had it spread out in front of her. And to Ella's dismay, her sister was dropping toast crumbs all over the pictures of holiday decorating ideas.

"There's a table setting in here, Ella, of china similar to Mother's." She held it up so her sister could see. "We should use ours more often."

"Mother always loved roses," Ella said. "Try not to spill anything on the magazine. I'm not through reading it yet."

"I won't," Lou promised, but Ella knew Lou was sure to dribble. She looked out the window and watched the snow fall once again. An early winter was nothing to get excited about, but the children in the neighborhood loved making snowmen in their yards on the days when school was canceled.

"I wonder if there's school today," she murmured. "The bus is late."

Louisa glanced up. "No, here it comes."

Sure enough, the bus lumbered into view and made its usual journey down Elm Street, though it seemed to be going faster than normal. To Ella's horror, Cameron's white Buick began to edge backward down his driveway.

"Oh, no," she cried. "He's going too fast. They both are."

"Who?" Lou didn't bother to put the magazine down.

"Stop, you old fool," Ella chanted, staring at a disaster in the making. "Stop, stop, *stop!*"

"Ella?" Louisa put down her teacup and stared at her twin. "What's going on?"

Ella winced, her heart in her throat. "We have to

dial 911. One of your boyfriends just crashed into the school bus."

TEN MINUTES BEFORE SHE was to meet her groom, Suzanne stood inside the town hall. The wide corridor outside the various town offices was cold, so she kept her coat buttoned and her gloves on. She didn't know if her teeth were chattering from cold or nerves or because her shoes had gotten wet when she'd walked across the snowy parking lot. She wasn't sure which was more hazardous, driving through town or trying to negotiate a slippery parking lot.

Two other couples waited outside the room with Justice of the Peace printed in gold block letters on the door. Precisely at eight-thirty, a young woman opened the door and asked who was first, so one of the nervous-looking couples disappeared inside, while the other bride and groom went to the other end of the corridor and began kissing. Suzanne sat on the bench in the corridor and looked at her watch.

She hoped last night's snow wouldn't delay Owen too long. By nine, couple number three arrived and went inside to be joined in holy matrimony. Suzanne unbuttoned her coat and hoped the ivory silk blouse hadn't wrinkled too much. By nine-fifteen she began to feel sick to her stomach. By nine-thirty she had suffered enough curious looks to last her a lifetime.

At nine thirty-five she went into the ladies' room and threw up. And by nine forty-six, after rinsing her mouth and splashing cold water on her face, and trying to breathe despite the pain in her heart, Suzanne had to admit that she had been left at the altar again.

Owen Chase, the cowboy who always kept his promises, had changed his mind.

OWEN WAS IN A PANIC. He held Melanie against his side and hurried as fast as he could down the crowded corridor toward the main desk.

"Where is she?" he asked yet another person he hoped could tell him anything at all. But before the young man in a blue lab coat could answer, Owen saw Callie behind the counter, and he hoped his prayers had been answered. "Callie! Thank goodness, can you tell me what's going on? Where is she?"

She looked up and met his gaze, then waved him over through the crowd. "Owen, it's all right. *She's* all right."

"But where is she?" He wouldn't believe everything was okay until he saw for himself.

"In with the doctor. I'll let you see her in a few minutes, as soon as he's done with the examination."

"But she's okay." He was out of breath, so he set Mel on the counter in front of him and held her there.

"Yes. I wouldn't lie to you. The kids are mostly

shook up, except for one broken arm and a few stitches here and there. I think the parents are in worse shape than the kids."

Owen could believe it. He'd never spent a worse hour in his life, from the time he got the phone call from the school principal informing him of "a semi-serious bus crash," to an endlessly long drive to the hospital in Barstow, to now, when relief and panic were threatening to make him physically ill.

"Owen?"

He didn't realize he'd closed his eyes until he lifted his head and opened them. Callie looked worried. "I'm okay. But I was supposed to get married this morning."

"Congratulations. Is the lucky lady that reporter?"

"Yes, if she's still speaking to me. Is there a phone around here I can use?"

"Here you go," she said, setting a telephone on the counter next to Melanie. "And after you're done, I'm going to give you some insurance forms to fill out while you wait to see Darcy."

"Thanks." Owen kept his arm around the baby and picked up the phone with his free hand before he realized he had no idea who to call. The clock on the wall behind the desk said nine forty-six, which meant Suzanne might still be at the town hall or she had returned to Blissful Nights B and B.

"Callie?"

"What?" She looked up from something she was reading.

"What's your grandmother's phone number?"

He dialed the number she told him and, as he listened to the busy signal from the other end of the line, Owen's panic increased. He needed to find Suzanne, who by now must think he'd run out on her. And he needed to see Darcy, who must be frightened half out of her mind.

Then there was another possibility—that Suzanne had decided not to marry him after all, and was on her way to Great Falls and out of his life.

"WELL, MISSY, how'd you make out here? Find a man or did a man find you?"

"Neither one." Suzanne tried to smile at the gas station attendant. She remembered Hal from last week—who could forget him? "Could you fill it up, please, Hal?"

"Well, sure." He went around to the side of the car and stuck in the gas nozzle, then came back and tapped on the window for her to roll it down again. "What happened? Last time I saw you was the night you were dancing with that Chase rancher."

"He left me at the altar," she said, assuming Hal would think she was joking. She was going to cry again if she had to say one more word.

"Well, well." He stared at her a little too long before hurrying off to take care of the car that drove up behind her. Suzanne grabbed another tissue from her bag. She really, really wished she could have gotten out of town without a conversation about her broken heart, but she didn't have anything to be ashamed of. Owen Chase was the one who'd backed out.

Suzanne blew her nose and wondered if she was cursed.

So far it had been a morning from hell. She'd returned Grace's blouse, changed her clothes, paid her bill and made Grace promise not to tell anyone what had happened—or not happened. She'd called the ranch and let the phone ring for what seemed like half an hour, and then Grace had made her take some sips of tea and a bite of toast.

And then, unwilling to prolong the embarrassment, Suzanne had said goodbye. She had already loaded her car with her suitcases, thinking she'd be going home with Owen after the wedding. It was a school day; they would have a honeymoon while Mel took a nap. Suzanne had never really believed he would change his mind, but the more she thought about it, the more she thought this might just be for the best. Darcy, grieving for her mother, wouldn't want an aunt, a stranger, in her life. Suzanne wouldn't allow herself to think about Melanie, who needed and deserved a mother.

"That'll be twenty-nine dollars even," Hal said, so Suzanne handed him her credit card and wiped her eyes. Maybe Owen wasn't as wonderful as he seemed. To hell with Bliss and its matchmaking silliness. She was going home to New York and never, ever believing another man again.

ELLA COULDN'T DIAL Grace's number fast enough. When her friend answered, she almost shrieked. "Hal just called me to say that Miss Greenway's at his station and on her way out of town. I thought you told me they were getting married!"

"They were." Grace sighed. "But he didn't meet her at the town hall, and she came back, then left."

"And you couldn't *stall* her?" Ella decided the whole world had gone mad. First the accident, which was practically in their front yard, and now Grace couldn't manage the smallest problem by herself.

"What's the matter?" Louisa asked, coming over to the phone. "Didn't they get married?"

"No," Ella snapped. "Owen didn't show up and our Miss Greenway has left town." She turned her attention back to Grace. "I'm putting you on speaker phone, Grace, so Lou can hear every word." She pushed the appropriate button. "Say something, Grace."

"I did my best, Ella," she sniffed. "I made tea and toast. I talked her into calling him, but there was no answer. I can't imagine where he would be. We know he's in love with her. Missy's here with me now and we were just trying to come up with—"

"The bus," Louisa told them. "Do you think Darcy Chase was on the bus that Cameron hit?"

"Possibly," Ella replied. "They thought that idiot Cam was a little shaky and they should check out his heart."

"What accident?" Grace cried, and Ella heard Missy's shriek in the background.

"Cameron hit the school bus," Louisa hollered. "His driveway was icy and so was the road, and everyone was going too fast—"

"Take a breath," Ella told her, "or you'll hyperventilate."

"They took all the students to the hospital," Louisa insisted. "In Barstow."

"And Owen Chase would have been called," Grace said, her relief audible. "So that's where he was. Oh, poor Suzanne."

"'Poor Suzanne' is at the gas station," Ella stated. "And we all know what *that* means."

They certainly did. Ella Bliss wasn't a matchmaker for nothing.

"SORRY, MISS," Hal said for the fifteenth time. "I don't know what's going on with our credit card machine."

Suzanne held out three ten-dollar bills. "I told you, Hal, I can pay cash."

He put his hands up. "Oh, no, I'm sure it will just be another minute. I've got one of the boys working on it now and we'll have it up and running in no time. We think it charged you, but we can't get the receipt out of the machine for you to sign."

"Well, okay, but I'd be glad to give you the money."

"Don't want to charge you twice," the old man said. "Wouldn't be right."

At least she had enough gas to keep the engine running and the heat on, though she didn't understand the problem with taking cash. He'd asked her to pull away from the gas pumps and park off to one side while she waited, so Suzanne had done precisely that. She watched the cars and trucks go past, heading into town, and saw several slide a little on the slick road. She didn't look forward to driving to Great Falls, but surely the main highway would be sanded and plowed.

Hal knocked on her window again, so Suzanne rolled down the glass and took the receipt he handed her, along with the pen. Once she'd signed the paper and he'd returned her card, Suzanne thanked him and said goodbye.

"Well, not so fast," Hal drawled. "There's some

folks who want to talk to you." He leaned closer. "I couldn't let you go home thinking we failed you now, could I?"

Her windows were fogged up, so Suzanne couldn't see who Hal was referring to. He stepped back so she could open the car door. What she saw made her want to cry all over again. Four gray-haired matchmakers struggled to climb out of a large gold sedan and then headed her way. Suzanne shut off her engine and stepped out of the Explorer into the cold, hurrying to meet the ladies halfway. The less steps they had to take across the icy blacktop the better.

"Did I forget something?" Suzanne asked, though she knew darn well she hadn't. Ella Bliss was in the lead, her thick black boots stomping along at a rapid pace as she avoided truck bumpers and clouds of exhaust. The other three hurried to keep up, but it was Ella whom Suzanne met first.

"You forgot your groom," the woman said.

"We know where he is," Louisa panted, her breath coming out in little white puffs as she caught up to her sister.

"I'm sure he meant to show up," Missy added. "Owen Chase would never go back on his word."

Grace nodded. "I think we've managed to solve the mystery, dear, and as soon as we find Owen the wedding can take place."

"I don't think this wedding was 'meant to be,' do you?" Then Suzanne realized who she was talking to. She and the ladies moved closer to the building as another truck pulled up to the pump and a door slammed shut.

"Oh, don't say that," Missy groaned. "We have our hearts set on this match."

Suzanne shivered. "I think it's for the best that I leave."

"Best for who?" Owen Chase came around the back of his truck. He looked tired and pale as he stepped closer, his beautiful mouth slanting down as if he was bracing himself for bad news. It was proving harder to get out of Bliss than she'd thought.

"Everybody," Suzanne replied, while the ladies tittered and waved to Darcy and Mel, who peered at them out of the open passenger window. "What are you doing here?"

"I just got back into town," he explained, meeting her gaze. "The first thing I see is your car, and you, and the ladies, here with Hal. What's going on?"

"I'm leaving," she said, hoping she sounded haughty and cold. She didn't want him to know he'd broken her heart.

"Without letting me explain?"

"You don't have to," she said, aware of their rapt audience. "We both had the right to change our minds. It was part of the agreement."

"I didn't change my mind," he growled. "Did you?"

"I waited an hour," she confessed, feeling tears sting her eyes once again. "Where were you?"

"It's all my fault, Suzanne, honest," Darcy cried out. "Uncle Owen, tell her about the bus and make her come home with us."

"Oh, yes," Ella said, while Louisa waved to the baby. "Tell her about the bus."

"Later," Owen said, ignoring all of them. He gathered Suzanne into his arms and she went, despite her better judgment. She should kick him in the shins and run to her car and get out of town, but he was big and solid and warm—and everything she'd ever wanted.

"I'm sorry," he whispered close to her ear. "There was an accident—"

"What?" She pulled away to look up at him, but he wrapped her in his embrace once again.

"It's fine now," he assured her. "But I missed our wedding, which I hated to do."

"You have until noon," Ella said, standing close to them so she wouldn't miss a word. "Plenty of time to get over to the town hall and get the job done."

"We could all go," Darcy added, and Suzanne realized the girl had a thick bandage on her forehead. "Like a *real* wedding."

"It'll be real, all right," Owen promised, his lips grazing her cheek. "And so will the honeymoon."

"This is so romantic," Louisa sighed. "But it's getting rather cold out here, don't you think?"

"Shh," the others said in unison.

"I will love you forever," Owen promised her. "Whether you marry me today or not."

"I love you, too," Suzanne admitted, much to the delight of the listeners. She lifted her head and looked up at him. "And I think we'd better get to the town hall before we all freeze to death."

Owen kissed her, a wonderfully warm kiss that promised a lifetime of passion. When they caught their breath, Suzanne looked around at their audience. Darcy made Melanie clap her fat palms together while the four matchmakers stood near them in a teary huddle.

"I think we're all crazy," she told them, but she smiled through her tears.

"These things happen here in Bliss, my dear." Ella Bliss reached over and patted her shoulder. "You may as well get used to living happily ever after."

_____Epilogue_____

"I DO SO LOVE WEDDINGS," Missy sniffed. She reached into her oversize handbag and pulled out a clump of tissues, which she distributed to the others. Louisa, tears running down her pudgy cheeks, thoughtfully reached over and wiped the baby's nose, a gesture which did not go unnoticed by her sister. A few feet away, towards the front of the oak-lined chamber the justice of the peace used for weddings, Owen Chase was pledging to love and honor Suzanne Greenway. 'Til death do them part.

"We all love weddings," Ella agreed, noting that Grace was surreptitiously wiping her eyes. Of the four members of the Hearts Club, Ella realized she was the only one not overcome by feelings of sentimentality. Triumphant, yes. Satisfied? Absolutely. And confident that this match would be a successful one, of course.

She didn't know what there was to cry about. Owen's teenage niece held the baby, who kept reaching for her uncle. The older girl looked happy, thank goodness.

"Lou," Ella whispered, leaning closer to her sister. "Do stop sniffling and get a hold of yourself."

"I can't—" she gasped for air "—help it. It's just so wonderful, don't you think?"

"Good grief," Ella muttered. She tried to catch Grace's eye, but Grace was busy taking another tissue from Missy.

"'Til death us do part," Suzanne announced, finishing her share of the vows.

"I now pronounce you husband and wife," the judge declared, to the great delight of all who observed him.

Ella watched the rancher bend down to kiss his red-haired wife. His boots were soaked, his hair mussed as if he'd run his fingers through it a hundred times. The bride wore black and the young maid-of-honor sported a thick bandage on her forehead and held a fat, squirming baby.

It was all very lovely, though Ella wished the bride looked a little more festive. But there'd been no sense in stopping to change clothes, not with time running out. And this particular bride and groom didn't need any more bad luck in their lives. What they needed was plenty of time to be in love, to live together in marital harmony, in the true Bliss tradition.

The Hearts Club would help in whatever way possible, Ella resolved. At least for today.

Tomorrow Ella would call a special meeting. She

would serve jasmine tea—thank goodness it had finally arrived—and discuss her ideas for Calder Brown and Gabe O'Connor, two men who needed help finding wives.

Ella smiled to herself before accepting Owen's thanks and kiss on the cheek. There was nothing she loved better than a happy ending.

* * * * *

Watch Out!
'Cause the Bliss ladies are
matchmaking again, and they're determined
to catch wild and sexy Calder Brown
and see him settled...
Don't miss Kristine Rolofson's exciting sequel in
the MONTANA MATCHMAKERS *miniseries:*
#850 A BRIDE FOR CALDER BROWN
available October 2001!

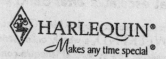

If you enjoyed what you just read,
then we've got an offer you can't resist!

Take 2 bestselling love stories FREE!

Plus get a FREE surprise gift!

Harlequin truly does make any time special. . . . This year we are celebrating weddings in style!

To help us celebrate, we want you to tell us how wearing the Harlequin wedding gown will make your wedding day special. As the grand prize, Harlequin will offer one lucky bride the chance to **"Walk Down the Aisle"** in the Harlequin wedding gown!

There's more...

For her honeymoon, she and her groom will spend five nights at the **Hyatt Regency Maui.** As part of this five-night honeymoon at the hotel renowned for its romantic attractions, the couple will enjoy a candlelit dinner for two in Swan Court, a sunset sail on the hotel's catamaran, and duet spa treatments.

Maui • Molokai • Lanai

To enter, please write, in, 250 words or less, how wearing the Harlequin wedding gown will make your wedding day special. The entry will be judged based on its emotionally compelling nature, its originality and creativity, and its sincerity. This contest is open to Canadian and U.S. residents only and to those who are 18 years of age and older. There is no purchase necessary to enter. Void where prohibited. See further contest rules attached. Please send your entry to:

Walk Down the Aisle Contest

In Canada	In U.S.A.
P.O. Box 637	P.O. Box 9076
Fort Erie, Ontario	3010 Walden Ave.
L2A 5X3	Buffalo, NY 14269-9076

You can also enter by visiting www.eHarlequin.com
Win the Harlequin wedding gown and the vacation of a lifetime!
The deadline for entries is October 1, 2001.

HARLEQUIN®
Makes any time special ®

PHWDACONT1

HARLEQUIN WALK DOWN THE AISLE TO MAUI CONTEST 1197
OFFICIAL RULES
NO PURCHASE NECESSARY TO ENTER

1. To enter, follow directions published in the offer to which you are responding. Contest begins April 2, 2001, and ends on October 1, 2001. Method of entry may vary. Mailed entries must be postmarked by October 1, 2001, and received by October 8, 2001.

2. Contest entry may be, at times, presented via the Internet, but will be restricted solely to residents of certain geographic areas that are disclosed on the Web site. To enter via the Internet, if permissible, access the Harlequin Web site (www.eHarlequin.com) and follow the directions displayed online. Online entries must be received by 11:59 p.m. E.S.T. on October 1, 2001.

   In lieu of submitting an entry online, enter by mail by hand-printing (or typing) on an 8½" x 11" plain piece of paper, your name, address (including zip code), Contest number/name and in 250 words or fewer, why winning a Harlequin wedding dress would make your wedding day special. Mail via first-class mail to: Harlequin Walk Down the Aisle Contest 1197, (in the U.S.) P.O. Box 9076, 3010 Walden Avenue, Buffalo, NY 14269-9076, (in Canada) P.O. Box 637, Fort Erie, Ontario L2A 5X3, Canada. Limit one entry per person, household address and e-mail address. Online and/or mailed entries received from persons residing in geographic areas in which Internet entry is not permissible will be disqualified.

3. Contests will be judged by a panel of members of the Harlequin editorial, marketing and public relations staff based on the following criteria:

   - Originality and Creativity—50%
   - Emotionally Compelling—25%
   - Sincerity—25%

   In the event of a tie, duplicate prizes will be awarded. Decisions of the judges are final.

4. All entries become the property of Torstar Corp. and will not be returned. No responsibility is assumed for lost, late, illegible, incomplete, inaccurate, nondelivered or misdirected mail or misdirected e-mail, for technical, hardware or software failures of any kind, lost or unavailable network connections, or failed, incomplete, garbled or delayed computer transmission or any human error which may occur in the receipt or processing of the entries in this Contest.

5. Contest open only to residents of the U.S. (except Puerto Rico) and Canada, who are 18 years of age or older, and is void wherever prohibited by law; all applicable laws and regulations apply. Any litigation within the Province of Quebec respecting the conduct or organization of a publicity contest may be submitted to the Régie des alcools, des courses et des jeux for a ruling. Any litigation respecting the awarding of a prize may be submitted to the Régie des alcools, des courses et des jeux only for the purpose of helping the parties reach a settlement. Employees and immediate family members of Torstar Corp. and D. L. Blair, Inc., their affiliates, subsidiaries and all other agencies, entities and persons connected with the use, marketing or conduct of this Contest are not eligible to enter. Taxes on prizes are the sole responsibility of winners. Acceptance of any prize offered constitutes permission to use winner's name, photograph or other likeness for the purposes of advertising, trade and promotion on behalf of Torstar Corp., its affiliates and subsidiaries without further compensation to the winner, unless prohibited by law.

6. Winners will be determined no later than November 15, 2001, and will be notified by mail. Winners will be required to sign and return an Affidavit of Eligibility form within 15 days after winner notification. Noncompliance within that time period may result in disqualification and an alternative winner may be selected. Winners of trip must execute a Release of Liability prior to ticketing and must possess required travel documents (e.g. passport, photo ID) where applicable. Trip must be completed by November 2002. No substitution of prize permitted by winner. Torstar Corp. and D. L. Blair, Inc., their parents, affiliates, and subsidiaries are not responsible for errors in printing or electronic presentation of Contest, entries and/or game pieces. In the event of printing or other errors which may result in unintended prize values or duplication of prizes, all affected game pieces or entries shall be null and void. If for any reason the Internet portion of the Contest is not capable of running as planned, including infection by computer virus, bugs, tampering, unauthorized intervention, fraud, technical failures, or any other causes beyond the control of Torstar Corp. which corrupt or affect the administration, secrecy, fairness, integrity or proper conduct of the Contest, Torstar Corp. reserves the right, at its sole discretion, to disqualify any individual who tampers with the entry process and to cancel, terminate, modify or suspend the Contest or the Internet portion thereof. In the event of a dispute regarding an online entry, the entry will be deemed submitted by the authorized holder of the e-mail account submitted at the time of entry. Authorized account holder is defined as the natural person who is assigned to an e-mail address by an Internet access provider, online service provider or other organization that is responsible for arranging e-mail address for the domain associated with the submitted e-mail address. **Purchase or acceptance of a product offer does not improve your chances of winning.**

7. Prizes: (1) Grand Prize—A Harlequin wedding dress (approximate retail value: $3,500) and a 5-night/6-day honeymoon trip to Maui, HI, including round-trip air transportation provided by Maui Visitors Bureau from Los Angeles International Airport (winner is responsible for transportation to and from Los Angeles International Airport) and a Harlequin Romance Package, including hotel accomodations (double occupancy) at the Hyatt Regency Maui Resort and Spa, dinner for (2) two at Swan Court, a sunset sail on Kiele V and a spa treatment for the winner (approximate retail value: $4,000); (5) Five runner-up prizes of a $1000 gift certificate to selected retail outlets to be determined by Sponsor (retail value $1000 ea.). Prizes consist of only those items listed as part of the prize. Limit one prize per person. All prizes are valued in U.S. currency.

8. For a list of winners (available after December 17, 2001) send a self-addressed, stamped envelope to: Harlequin Walk Down the Aisle Contest 1197 Winners, P.O. Box 4200 Blair, NE 68009-4200 or you may access the www.eHarlequin.com Web site through January 15, 2002.

Contest sponsored by Torstar Corp., P.O. Box 9042, Buffalo, NY 14269-9042, U.S.A.

PHWDACONT2

In August look for

AN IDEAL MARRIAGE?

by *New York Times* bestselling author

DEBBIE MACOMBER

A special 3-in-1 collector's edition containing
three full-length novels from America's favorite
storyteller, Debbie Macomber—each ending
with a delightful walk down the aisle.

Father's Day
First Comes Marriage
Here Comes Trouble

Evoking all the emotion and warmth
that you've come to expect from
Debbie, AN IDEAL MARRIAGE?
will definitely satisfy!

DON'T MISS OUT!

MONTANA MAVERICKS: BIG SKY GROOMS
Three brand-new historical stories about the Kincaids,
Montana's most popular family

RETURN TO WHITEHORN, MONTANA—
WHERE LEGENDS ARE BEGUN AND
LOVE LASTS FOREVER BENEATH THE BIG SKY....

Available in August 2001

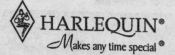

Makes any time special ®

Visit us at www.eHarlequin.com

PHBSGR

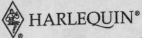